D1143272

101 123 998 58

Injury Time

WHO POISONED Anna Macmillan with a deadly dose of antimony? What caused the temperature of a health club sauna to rise so dramatically that its occupant was dead within minutes? Where are the priceless pearls which vanished during a country house weekend and how was the code to an eminent scientist's high-tech alarm system broken on the day it was issued?

From the idiosyncratic investigations of the phlegmatic D.I. Sloan and his enthusiastic Constable Crosby in the police station down in the not-so-sleepy county of Calleshire to the long lunches of civil servant Henry Tyler in the tranquil environs of London's Mordaunt Club, Catherine Aird's collection of sixteen short stories takes the reader through an ingenious selection of crimes and puzzles, full of delightful literary subtleties and fascinating legal and medical information. Written with the deftest of touches and plenty of wit, *Injury Time* makes it obvious why Catherine Aird was awarded the Crime Writers' Association's Golden Handcuffs Award – 'for giving much pleasure over many years'.

BY THE SAME AUTHOR

The Religious Body

A Most Contagious Game

Henrietta Who?

The Complete Steel

A Late Phoenix

His Burial Too

Slight Mourning

Parting Breath

Some Die Eloquent

Passing Strange

Last Respects

Harm's Way

A Dead Liberty

The Body Politic

A Going Concern

CATHERINE AIRD

Injury Time

WANDSWORTH PUBLIC LIBRARIES

M

MACMILLAN

LONDON

101123998

This collection first published 1994 by Macmillan London Limited

a division of Pan Macmillan Publishers Limited
Cavaye Place London SW10 9PG
and Basingstoke

Associated companies throughout the world

ISBN 0-333-62589-7

All stories © Catherine Aird

Steady as she Goes © 1992; this story first appeared
in *First Culprit* (Chatto & Windus, 1992)
The Man Who Rowed for the Shore © 1992; this story first appeared in
The Man Who . . . Anthology (Macmillan, 1992)
A Fair Cop © 1994
Jeopardy © 1994
Lord Peter's Touch © 1990; this story first appeared in
Encounters with Lord Peter (The Dorothy Sayers Society, 1990)
Memory Corner © 1994
Slight of Hand © 1993; this story first appeared in
Second Culprit (Chatto & Windus, 1993)
Cause and Effects © 1990; this story first appeared in
A Classic English Crime (Pavilion Books, 1990)
The Hard Sell © 1994
One Under the Eight © 1994
Bare Essentials © 1994
Home is the Hunter © 1988; this story first appeared in
the *Crime Writers' Association Anthology* (Gollancz, 1988)
Blue Upright © 1994
Devilled Dip © 1994
The Misjudgement of Paris © 1994
Her Indoors © 1994

The right of Catherine Aird to be identified as the
author of this work has been asserted by her in accordance
with the Copyright, Designs and Patents Act 1988.

All rights reserved. No reproduction, copy or transmission
of this publication may be made without written permission.
No paragraph of this publication may be reproduced, copied or
transmitted save with written permission or in accordance with
the provisions of the Copyright Act 1956 (as amended). Any
person who does any unauthorized act in relation to
this publication may be liable to criminal prosecution
and civil claims for damages.

1 3 5 7 9 8 6 4 2

A CIP catalogue record for this book is available from
the British Library

Phototypeset by Intype, London
Printed by Mackays of Chatham PLC, Chatham, Kent

For Brian

in appreciation

Contents

Steady as she Goes

'THE FACTS OF THE MATTER,' declared Superintendent Leeyes, 'are quite simple.'

Detective Inspector Sloan waited without saying anything. In fact, had there happened to have been a salt-cellar handy in the Superintendent's office in Berebury Police Station he might very well have taken a pinch from it. In his experience, open-and-shut cases seldom came his way anyway and never if the Superintendent had had a hand in matters to date.

'The deceased,' said Leeyes, 'died from poisoning by antimony.' He grunted and added, 'According to Dr Dabbe, that is.'

Sloan made a note. In his book, if not in the Superintendent's, that constituted a solid fact. Dr Dabbe was the Consultant Pathologist for their half of the County of Calleshire and not a man to say antimony when he meant arsenic.

'The doctor,' swept on Leeyes, who was inclined to treat medical pronouncements as the starting point for discussion rather than the end of it, 'says in his report that the Reinsch test was positive for antimony.'

Detective Inspector Sloan made another note. By rights it was Detective Constable Crosby sitting by his side who should have been taking the notes but unfortunately as it happened the detective constable actually was a man to write alimony when he meant antimony and Sloan thought

1

in a case of poisoning it was better to be on the safe side and do it himself.

'The deceased's sister,' growled the Superintendent, 'alleges that the poison was administered by the husband . . .'

'Most murderers are widowers,' remarked Detective Inspector Sloan, that most happily married of men. 'And certainly almost all male murderers are.'

The Superintendent rose effortlessly above the Home Office's statistics. 'And,' he continued with heavy irony, 'the husband is insisting that the sister did it.'

'Hasn't that got a funny name, sir?' Detective Constable Crosby's wayward attention seemed to have been engaged at last.

'Funny!' barked the Superintendent. 'Since when, may I ask, has there been anything funny about murder?'

'Not murder itself, sir,' responded Crosby earnestly. 'I meant that I thought that the word for that sort of murder was a funny one.'

'Murder is always murder,' Leeyes was at his most majestic, 'whatever Defence Counsel chooses to call it at the trial.'

Detective Inspector Sloan's hobby was growing roses and he was just thinking about the parallel where they smelt as sweet by any other name when Crosby put his oar in again.

'They said so, sir,' persisted the Detective Constable with all the innocence of youth, 'at the Training College.'

'Fratricide,' managed Leeyes between clenched teeth. Older and wiser men than Crosby knew better than to mention Police Training College to the Superintendent. Not only was the very concept an anathema to him but there was nothing in his view better than the time-honoured walking the beat with a sergeant or 'sitting next to Nellie' way of learning.

'But that's when you kill your brother, isn't it, sir?' persisted Crosby. 'Shouldn't it be "sorocide" if it's your sister? Or is that satricide?'

'The word "homicide" will do, Crosby,' interposed Detective Inspector Sloan swiftly before either of the other two thought about the killing of satyrs – or kings, come to that. He enquired if such a thing as a motive for the poisoning existed.

'According to the sister, yes. According to the husband, no.'

'Gain?' suggested Sloan, veteran of many a domestic murder. So far the case hadn't struck him as 'open-and-shut' in any way at all.

'The love of money is the root of all evil,' quoted the Superintendent sententiously.

This seemed to be the view, too, of Miss Kirsty McCormack, sister of the late Mrs Anna Macmillan.

She was a thin, rather dowdy woman, with thick glasses, living in a modest bungalow set in a very large garden on the outskirts of Berebury. Miss McCormack seemed only too anxious to talk to the two policemen.

'We came here about twelve years ago, Inspector, Mother and I,' she said, ushering them into a preternaturally neat and tidy sitting-room. 'Won't you sit over there, Constable? On the settee. Inspector, I think you'd be more comfortable in Mother's old chair by the fire.'

'Thank you, miss.' Sloan could not think at first what it was that was so odd about the room and then it came to him. All the walls were bare. There was a not a picture or a photograph to be seen.

'It was after her first heart attack that we moved. We thought she would be better not having to climb the stairs.'

'You've got rather a lot of land, though,' observed Sloan, no mean gardener.

'Indeed, yes, although as you can see I had to let it go.'
She sighed. 'The garden is part of the trouble.'

'Upkeep?' suggested Sloan, not unsympathetically. 'It would be considerable.'

'Oh, no, Inspector. It's much too big even to try to keep it up without help. Besides, I was too busy looking after Mother, especially towards the end.'

'Quite so, miss.' He waited. 'And . . .'

'And then Mother died,' she said flatly.

Sloan coughed. 'She can't have been young.'

'She wasn't. I decided to move – there was a dear little flat on the market in Calleford and I'd always wanted to live over there.'

'A very pretty city,' said Sloan, who would have found it stifling himself.

'That's when the trouble started.'

'Trouble?' Sloan's head came up like that of an old war-horse and even Crosby looked faintly interested.

'We found that this dreadful old garden was just what the developers had been looking for.'

'I see, miss.' Detective Inspector Sloan, husband and father, who had to think carefully each autumn how many new roses he could afford to add to his collection, wasn't sure that he did.

'Anna and I suddenly became rather well off,' she said.

This time Sloan thought he was beginning to under-stand. 'You and your sister were co-heirs, I take it?'

'That's right, Inspector.' She looked him squarely in the eye. 'So Paul had quite a lot to gain from killing Anna.'

'Her share of your mother's estate,' hazarded Sloan, 'would come to him in the ordinary way should his wife die?'

'Exactly,' said Miss McCormack. A glint of amusement crossed her flinty features.

'Unless she had willed it to you,' pointed out Sloan.

'She hadn't,' said Miss McCormack. 'If Paul outlived her it was to go to him.'

There was a small movement from the direction of the settee. 'And if he didn't?' asked Detective Constable Crosby.

'It came to me.' There was no mistaking the sardonic amusement in Miss McCormack's expression now. 'There are no children, you see.' She gave a wintry smile and said, 'Paul, of course, insists that the same argument about gain applies to me.'

'And does it?' enquired Sloan.

'Either Paul would have to be found guilty of Anna's murder or I would have had to kill them both to inherit.'

On the settee Detective Constable Crosby stirred. 'And did you try?'

All trace of amusement vanished from Miss McCormack's face and she looked merely sad and weary. 'No, Constable, I didn't. And I don't know either how Paul killed Anna but I can tell you one thing. He did it before my very eyes and I can't for the life of me think how.'

'Perhaps,' said Detective Inspector Sloan, falling back on formality, 'you would tell us about the day in question . . . ?'

'I'd gone over to their house after tea – not that they were tea drinkers – at about a quarter past five. Paul was there but Anna hadn't come home from the hairdressers' – she was a bit later back than she expected. The traffic's always pretty bad then, you know.'

'We know,' said Sloan moderately.

'Paul said he'd only just got back from the office and he hadn't been home in the middle of the day because he'd had a business luncheon.'

'So there was no way that he could have given his wife

5

any poison before you came?' said Crosby. 'Is that what you mean?'

They hadn't, apparently, taught the Detective Constable at the Police Training College anything about not accepting statements by interested parties at face value but Sloan let that pass for the time being.

'Exactly,' said Miss McCormack as if to a promising pupil. 'Anyway, Anna came in just then, very smart from the hairdressers' and with loads of shopping, and said she was dying for a drink.'

'And die she did,' said Crosby incorrigibly.

Sloan decided that there was perhaps something to be said for the 'sitting next to Nellie' school of learning after all. No self-respecting mentor would have let him get away with that.

'Paul asked me what I would have and I asked for a dry ginger ale . . .'

'You were driving, miss?' said Sloan. He would deal with Crosby in the privacy of the police car later.

'No, Inspector, I don't drive. I'm teetotal but,' again the steely glint of amusement, 'I think you could say that Paul and Anna weren't.'

'I see, miss. And then?'

'Paul asked Anna what she would like and she asked for a Black Cat.'

'A black cat?' Sloan wrote that down rather doubtfully.

'Paul said she wasn't to call it that. Its proper name was *pousse-café*. Naturally I asked what it was and Anna said it was a cocktail that Paul had been practising.'

Even the soi-disant detective sitting on the settee pricked up his ears at that.

'Paul,' continued Miss McCormack, 'said that he'd found the recipe in an old book of drinks and Anna and he rather liked it. In fact he said he'd have one too and was

6

I sure I wouldn't change my mind about the ginger ale.'

'And did you, miss?'

'Certainly not, Inspector. I never touch alcohol and it's just as well I didn't because I'm sure that's how he killed her.'

'With the Black Cat?' Sloan sat back and thought hard. In his file were statements from the Scenes of Crimes Officer and the Forensic Science people that none of the bottles in the Macmillans' drinks cabinet contained antimony.

'With the *pousse-café*. Anna said she liked the Rainbow one best.' Miss McCormack pursed her lips and said, 'What I can't get over is that he must have poisoned her while I was watching him. He even told me what he was putting in it as he made it.'

'And can you remember, miss?'

'He started with grenadine syrup which is red and then maraschino . . . white.'

Sloan made a note. 'Then . . .'

'*Crème de menthe.*'

'That's green,' said Sloan confidently. 'After that . . .'

'Yellow Chartreuse. I remember that particularly because Paul couldn't find it to begin with and Anna said she was sure there was a full bottle of Chartreuse somewhere.'

'And was there?' Sloan had a list but he wasn't going to consult it. Not here and now. Nor his notes on the very high solubility of potassium antimony tartrate crystals.

'Yes, but it was green Chartreuse and that wouldn't have done because of the *crème de menthe*, you see.'

'No, miss. I don't see. You'll have to tell me why it wouldn't have done.'

'The Rainbow *pousse-café* is made up of drinks of all different colours,' said Miss McCormack. 'They're in the glass together but in layers.'

'Neapolitan,' said the over-grown school boy on the settee decisively.

'All you need is a steady hand,' she said. 'And you get a striped drink.'

'Did your brother-in-law find the yellow Chartreuse?' asked Sloan.

'Oh, yes, in the end,' said Miss McCormack. 'And the orange curaçao and the cognac.'

'What colour is cognac?' enquired Crosby.

'Amber. That was last.' She looked up. 'I must say the two glasses looked quite pretty standing there.'

'Forever Amber,' said Crosby.

'And then?' said Sloan, taking no notice.

'And then they drank them.'

'Both of them?'

'That is the interesting thing,' agreed Miss McCormack. 'Yes, Paul drank his, too.'

'Like the dog that didn't bark in the night,' said Crosby. He was ignored.

'And you are quite sure, miss, that exactly the same – er – ingredients went into each drink?'

'Quite sure,' said Miss McComack firmly. 'I tell you, I saw them made and the same amount came out of each bottle. Anyway, Paul let Anna choose the one she wanted herself.'

'Then what happened?' asked Sloan.

'We sat chatting while they drank their *pousse-cafés*. You obviously have to do it very slowly or the rainbow effect is spoilt.'

'Yes, miss.'

'We must have been sitting there for – oh, the best part of half an hour, Inspector, when the phone went. Paul went to answer it – he hoped it would be the garage to say that his car was ready after servicing. He came back presently to say that it was and he was just slipping out to collect it before the garage closed at six.'

'And then?'

For the first time Miss McCormack's composure crumpled. 'Anna got up and took the empty glasses out to the kitchen and then I heard her start vomiting – just ordinarily at first and then really violently.'

Detective Inspector Sloan had all the information he needed about the lethal effects of antimony in his file too but he still listened to the woman in front of him.

'By the time Paul came back poor Anna was in a pretty bad way with stomach cramps. He rang the doctor and they got her into hospital but she died that night in terrible pain.'

Sloan listened even more attentively to the distressed woman before him and then, policeman first and policeman second, said, 'What happened to the empty glasses?'

'They were found on the draining board in the kitchen afterwards, washed and upside-down. I think Anna must have done that before she started being ill.'

Sloan nodded. The police had gone to the house before Paul Macmillan had left the hospital and found no antimony anywhere but he did not say so to the woman in front of him.

'And neither you nor your brother-in-law was taken ill as well?' asked Sloan, although he knew already that antimony wasn't one of those poisons to which you build up a tolerance with low doses.

'Right as ninepence, both of us,' responded Miss McCormack. 'I understand,' she went on spiritedly, 'that Paul is alleging that I poisoned Anna after he had left to pick up his car.'

'I haven't spoken to him yet,' said Sloan diplomatically. 'We're on our way there now . . .'

Once back in the police car, though, Sloan told Crosby to drive only as far as the nearest lay-by. The two policemen sat there for some time while Detective Inspector Sloan sat and thought and Detective Constable Crosby to all intents and purposes just sat.

Eventually Detective Inspector Sloan pulled out the list of the contents of the drinks cabinet *chez* Macmillan and studied it carefully.

'What was it you said about the dog that didn't bark in the night, Crosby?'

'That it was interesting,' said the Constable. 'It's a quotation.'

'Would you say a bottle of grenadine that wasn't there was interesting, too?'

'Sir?'

'Never mind. Let's go and arrest Paul Macmillan for the murder of his wife, Anna.'

'How did he do it, then, sir?' Crosby let the clutch in at speed. If there was one thing in the world that he really liked it was driving fast cars fast.

'He put the antimony in the grenadine syrup beforehand and waited until his sister-in-law or some equally good witness came at drinks time. She was the best bet because she was both teetotal and short-sighted. Admirable characteristics, Crosby, if you propose murdering your wife by cocktail.'

'But Miss McCormack doesn't drink, sir.'

'Exactly. He knew she wouldn't accept a *pousse-café* or any other barbarically named alcoholic concoction. He could count on it.'

'What about the short sight?'

'I'm coming to that. He makes the cocktail up before her very eyes as the conjurors say and lets his wife choose hers. It doesn't matter which glass she chooses because they've both got antimony in . . .'

'But, sir . . .'

'But remember he knows there's antimony in his and his wife doesn't know that there's antimony in hers.'

'So . . .'

'So she drinks hers to the very last drop.'

'And he doesn't?'

'You can bet your life he doesn't, Crosby. He leaves the bottom layer.'

'The grenadine syrup?'

'Exactly. Put in first according to the recipe because it has got the highest specific gravity of all the constituents and thus stays at the bottom of the glass.'

'Where he leaves it?'

'Exactly. That was made much easier for him by the telephone ringing when it did – I dare say we shall find out when we ask that he arranged for the call from the garage as late in the day before they closed as possible. It gave him the excuse to leave the last of his drink untouched.'

'But what about the rest of the grenadine syrup?' asked Crosby, taking the corner at a speed that took insufficient account of centrifugal force.

'I think we shall find that went into his pocket while his back was to the two women and that it got lost on the way to or from the garage.'

'Like the Superintendent said, sir,' said Crosby going through the gears, 'it was an "open-and-shut" case then after all.'

'Well,' said Sloan modestly, 'I think you might say it was really more a matter of knowing exactly where the rainbow ends.'

The Man Who Rowed for the Shore

NORMAN PACE only made one mistake when he murdered his wife. That was to engage Horace Boller of the estuary village of Edsway and his boat *The Nancy* for the final disposal at sea of Millicent Pace's ashes. Norman didn't know, of course, at the time he did it, that hiring Horace Boller's motorboat would be his only mistake.

By the time he came to do so he thought – and with good reason – that all danger of detection was well and truly past and that he would very soon be able to give the nubile young lady in Personnel – she who saw no distinction, semantic or otherwise, between Personnel and Personal – more of his attention than would have been prudent as a married man.

Besides which he was then considering something which had turned out to be an unexpected problem. If anyone had told him beforehand that the main discussion point with his wife's family attendant upon her murder would be a sartorial one he would have laughed aloud; had he been the sort of man who laughed aloud – which he wasn't.

The right clothes – rather, the correct ones – to wear for the ceremony of casting Millicent's ashes into the sea had considerably exercised the mind of her brother, Graham Burnett, too. In fact the two men even discussed the matter at length – oddly enough it was manifest that the two brothers-in-law were on friendlier terms now than they had been before Millicent's death.

This was no accident. Norman had realized very early on that his main danger of detection in the murder would come from Millicent's brother Graham – a chartered accountant with a mind trained to expect cupidity in those with whom he dealt, money bringing out the best in nobody at all. In the little matter of averting his brother-in-law's possible suspicions Norman Pace felt he had been really rather clever . . .

First of all, as all the good books suggested in the matter of winning support from those whom you have reason to suppose do not like you, he had asked Graham a favour. Taking him quietly aside after luncheon on Christmas Day he had said: 'I wonder, old man, if I might put you down as one of my executors? I've got to go over to the States in the spring for the firm and I thought I'd tidy up my affairs first. I've never really enjoyed flying and you never know these days, do you?'

'Of course.' If Graham Burnett was surprised at the request his professionalism was far too ingrained for him to let surprise show in his face. 'Only too happy to help.'

'I know you'd look after Millicent anyway if anything happened to me,' he had said, 'and so it seemed easier to make it all legal.'

'Much better,' said the accountant firmly.

'By the way,' he had murmured as they had rejoined their respective wives, 'will you remember, if anything does happen, that I want to be cremated – we both do, actually.'

'I shan't forget,' promised Graham Burnett.

And he hadn't.

When Millicent Pace had died while Norman was safely in America, Graham had arranged for his sister to be cremated – as Norman had been sure he would. The fact that Norman was not able to be contacted in the United States of America at the critical moment was also the result of some careful forward planning. After his business was done,

Norman had set off for Milwaukee to visit a second cousin there.

Actually the second cousin wasn't there because he had died the year before but Norman had carefully neither mentioned the fact nor acknowledged the letter apprising him of it. Just before the time that he had calculated that Millicent would have died he checked out of his New York hotel without leaving a forwarding address and set off for Milwaukee. That he chose to do the journey by long-distance bus would, he knew, come as no surprise to his wife's family, among whom he had a fairly well-deserved reputation for being 'ower careful with the bawbees'.

His colleagues would not have been unduly surprised by his economy either. Always very attentive to his expenses claims, he was more than inclined to parsimony when it came to subscription lists and whip-rounds at work. In fact the only person either at work or among his family and friends who might have been surprised at his frugality was the nubile young lady in Personnel upon whom he had already lavished several gifts – but then she had been brought up by her mother on the well-attested aphorism that it was better to be an old man's darling than a young's man's slave . . .

In the United States Norman had been written off very early as a tight-wad, and it was this knowledge of his basic meanness which had led his brother-in-law Graham to turn down the undertaker's offer to keep Millicent Pace's body in a refrigerator until her husband's return. Finding out what it had cost to leave the coffin in the Chapel of Rest (Graham Burnett suspected that most of the time this was the shed at the back of the undertaker's yard) had already seriously alarmed him. As an accountant he was accustomed to breaking bad financial news and he did not relish it. The prospect of adding fiduciary complaint to Norman's personal grief did not appeal to him at all and he accordingly took the responsibility for arranging his sister's prompt cremation – as Norman had been sure he would.

On his visibly distressed return from Milwaukee, via New York where sad messages had awaited him, Norman Pace had listened to a long account of illness and death with suitable mien.

'I can assure you, Norman, everything that could be done was done,' said Graham in careful, neutral – but unctuous – tones that he could only have picked up from the undertaker.

'The doctor . . .' said an apparently broken-hearted Norman.

'He was marvellous,' said Graham swiftly. 'He couldn't do enough for poor Millicent.'

Norman had bowed his head. 'I'm glad to hear it.' In fact his brother-in-law had never said a truer word. The only thing the old fool had been able to do for Millicent had been to write her death certificate. The really important thing was that he had not associated any of her symptoms – abdominal pain and vomiting leading to heart failure – with poisoning by thallium.

Even more importantly, neither he, nor the other doctor who subsequently also signed the cremation certificate, had associated those everyday symptoms with Norman, by then in faraway Milwaukee. One of the undoubted attractions of thallium as a poison was the valuable delay in the onset of symptoms – it could be as long as forty-eight hours – as well as the peerless advantages of its being odourless, tasteless and colourless.

The only drawback of thallium known to Norman was that it was not only detectable in bone after death but that it survived in cremated ashes too. The disposal of Millicent's ashes at sea thus became more than mere ceremony.

Graham Burnett and his wife, not being privy to the real reason for the scattering of the ashes at sea, saw it only as an occasion. Hence the discussion about what to wear.

'I'm hoping for good weather, of course,' said Norman, 'but don't forget that it's always colder at sea than ashore.'

'That's what Neil says too,' said Graham. Neil was his son, a bright lad with all the cleverness of a born clown. 'I don't know about you, Norman, but even so I don't think a yellow sou'wester is quite right.'

'No,' agreed Norman, adding judiciously, 'but then neither is my black. Not at sea.'

'I hope you won't mind,' said Graham, 'but Neil says he's going to wear his cagoule.'

'I think,' said Norman with unaccustomed magnanimity, 'that everyone should put on whatever they feel most comfortable in.'

'So shall we say that dignified yet practical wear is the order of the day?' said Graham Burnett, who liked summing up.

Horace Boller, boatman, wore his usual working clothes for the expedition. Whether he knew it or not the fisherman's jersey which he had on complied with a long tradition of Aran knitting where each seaman's jersey was of a slightly different pattern, the better to identify the drowned.

Horace's deplorable garment could have been confused with no one else's – dead or alive. Norman Pace regarded him and his cluttered boat with distaste.

'You do understand, don't you, that we must be outside the three-mile territorial limit before it is legal for me to scatter my wife's ashes in the sea?' said Norman, who had his own reasons for being well out to sea before unscrewing the flask containing the mortal remains of Millicent. The said flask was nestling safely in the inner pocket of the new raincoat which Norman had seen fit to purchase for the occasion.

'Leave it to me, guv'nor,' said Boller, whose regard for the letter of the law was minimal and for its spirit non-existent. 'And watch that bit of coaming as you come aboard, if you don't mind. I've been having a peck of trouble with it. Now, be very careful . . .'

Conversation on board, stilted to begin with, thawed a little as Boller's boat turned out into the estuary from Edsway and headed for the open sea and Neil Burnett revealed himself as knowledgeable about birds.

'Common sandpiper,' he said in response to a question from his mother. She had settled on a tasteful grey outfit with plastic raincoat handy. 'And that's a ringed plover.'

'I suppose that one's a little twit,' said Angela, Neil's fiancée, who had insisted on joining the party to underline her new status as a potential member of the Burnett family. She, too, was wearing a cagoule.

Family solidarity on Norman's side was represented by two late-middle-aged sisters who were his cousins. Old enough to be veteran funeral-goers and therefore experienced mourners, they were kitted out in dark slacks and blazers left over from a Mediterranean cruise of long ago.

'I think it's a silly little goose,' responded Neil, giving Angela a quick hug.

This by-play on the part of the young ostensibly passed Norman Pace by, although he was obscurely gratified by the presence of Enid and Dora, who had not heard about the cremation in time to attend. He had taken up a rather aloof stance at the prow of the boat, looking out to sea, and letting his back give every appearance of a man thinking his own thoughts – if not actually communing with the deep. Horace Boller very nearly spoilt this tableau vivant by opening the throttle of the motor boat without warning just at the moment when they left the salt-marsh estuary behind and hit the open sea.

'Tide on the turn, I expect,' said Graham Burnett knowledgeably. He audited the books of several fishing enterprises in Kinnisport and thus felt qualified to give an opinion.

'Why are we going east and not straight out to sea?' demanded Norman, who was more observant.

'Got to get the church at Marby juxta Mare in line while I can still see Cranberry Point, haven't I,' said Horace Boller glibly. He paused, craftily waiting for the contradiction which would indicate that anyone on board *The Nancy* knew anything about nautical miles. It was not forthcoming so he went on, 'Otherwise I shan't know exactly how far out I am, shall I?'

Norman turned back to the bow. He'd struck a hard bargain with Boller but he didn't want the fisherman telling the whole party so. Horace Boller was still smarting from it, though, and had no intention of going half a mile further out to sea than he could get away with.

When he had gone nearly as far from land as he deemed necessary Horace put *The Nancy* about just enough to make the motor boat pitch fractionally. Mrs Burnett was the first to notice.

'It isn't going to get rough, is it?' she asked timorously. 'I'm not a very good sailor.'

Horace Boller throttled the engine back before grunting non-committally.

One of the effects of slowing the motorboat's speed was that it also began to roll ever so slightly.

Cousin Enid unfortunately chose to be bracing. 'Remember the Bay of Biscay, Dora, that time we were on our way back from Lisbon?'

'Don't remind me,' pleaded Dora. 'It was dreadful, simply dreadful.'

Horace Boller went through a charade of examining the sea and sky and looking anxious. He reduced the speed of the motorboat until it was scarcely making any headway at all, saving fuel the while.

'Haven't we gone far enough?' said Graham Burnett.

'Distances at sea are very deceptive,' observed Cousin Enid. 'It's always further than you think.'

'And later,' hissed Neil irrepressibly to Angela.

Norman Pace, standing in the prow, was aware that the boat was now beginning to wallow in the water. He patted the flask containing the ashes. How right he had been not to scatter them on land where they might one day have been sought by a diligent constabulary. Strewing them on the waves met every possible requirement . . .

'Should be all right now,' said Boller. 'Can't see St Peter's spire at Collerton any more.'

That this was because it was behind the headland he did not see fit to explain. Instead he put *The Nancy* about, switched off the engine and suggested to Norman that he came and stood at the lee side. 'Can't strew ashes into wind, can you?' said Boller grumpily. 'They'll only blow back at you.'

Nothing loath, Norman clambered back into the well of the boat and then, helped by Graham, stepped up on to the seating which ran round the inside of the tiny deck. He took out the flask from the crematorium, still slightly disconcerted that that fine white dust could contain all that had come between him and the young lady from Personnel.

'Steady as she goes,' quipped Neil unnecessarily. The nautical *double entendre* went unappreciated, all eyes being on Norman as he held the flask between his hands for a decent moment before unscrewing it. Enid and Dora, he was happy to see were standing at attention – at least as far as they were able to in the rocking boat.

In fact, Cousin Enid, always game, appeared to be saying

some private prayer – for which Norman was grateful since he found no words coming spontaneously to his own lips and the silence was a bit unnerving.

It was unfortunate that just as Enid had got to 'Eternal Father, Strong to save, whose arm doth bind the restless wave . . .' a very restless wave indeed caught *The Nancy* amidships. It was even more unfortunate that this happened just as Norman was about to unscrew the flask containing Millicent.

He lost his footing and the flask at the same moment.

'Butterfingers,' murmured young Neil, not quite *sotto voce* enough.

'Oh, my God!' said Norman, losing his cool as well as his footing and the flask, which was now bobbing briskly away from the stationary boat.

'It's not God's fault,' said Dora quietly in the eminently reasonable tones that must have accounted for the deaths – should they have used them, too – of quite a number of Early Christian Martyrs. On religious matters her docility was always trouble-making.

Any naval disciplinary court would have had no difficulty in holding Horace Boller – rather than God – to blame since he should never have allowed the boat to drift in the sort of sea he did, being, amongst other things, a hazard to shipping. As Their Lordships of the Admiralty were not called upon to pay for Horace's fuel – and he was – he remained untroubled.

Until, that is, Norman turned on him. 'Quick, start the engine . . . Look, it's floating about . . . just there. Hurry, man, hurry, or we'll lose her.'

With maddening calm Horace Boller applied himself to the engine. Everyone else on board rushed to the port side of *The Nancy*.

'Mind that coaming!' shouted Boller.

'Never mind your blasted coaming,' shouted back Norman, who had turned a nasty shade of puce. 'Get that engine going. Quickly, quickly . . . keep your eyes on her, everyone.'

The engine of the motorboat gave a little cough and then reluctantly sprang to life.

'Follow that flask . . .' Norman implored Boller urgently.

'Yoicks! Tally ho!' said Neil.

'Neil, you are awful,' said Angela.

'She went that way . . .' said Norman since the flask could now be seen only intermittently bobbing on the waves

'That way,' said Cousin Dora, pointing in a different direction.

'She's over there,' said Graham's wife distantly. She'd always rather liked her sister-in-law and thought the whole expedition unseemly.

'Where?' Norman clutched her arm. 'Which way?'

Graham Burnett said nothing at all: but his brother-in-law's patent dismay gave him furiously to think.

So did his next exchange with Boller.

'What sort of a tide is it?' Norman demanded, advancing on the boatman.

'Flow,' said Boller testily. 'Now, which way is it you want me to go?'

It was too late. Of the little flask containing the mortal remains of Millicent there was now nothing whatsoever to be seen.

'If we don't catch her,' Norman asked the fisherman, 'where will she fetch up?'

'*De profundis*,' murmured Enid.

'Dead man's reach,' whispered Neil to Angela, who gave him a little shove in response.

'Billy's Finger,' said Boller without hesitation. 'Spit of shingle in the estuary where the tide turns . . .'

'A dead spit . . .' murmured Neil in Angela's ear.

'You'll find her there by morning, guv'nor,' promised Boller. 'No problem.'

There was a problem, though.

For Norman, anyway.

Millicent's ashes had indeed fetched up on Billy's Finger in the estuary of the river Calle by morning but then so had Detective Inspector Sloan and Detective Constable Crosby, advised (Graham Burnett would never have used the expression 'tipped off') by Millicent's brother that there might be a message for them in a bottle.

There was.

As Millicent, his late wife, would have said, it was just like Norman to spoil the ship for a ha'p'orth of tar.

A Fair Cop

'I DON'T BELIEVE IT,' said Inspector Harpe flatly. 'I just don't believe it.'

'It's true, Harry,' said Detective Inspector Sloan.

'It's no good. You'll have to pull the other one,' said Inspector Harpe, who was from Berebury Constabulary's Traffic Division. He was known throughout the Calleshire County Force as Happy Harry because he had never been seen to smile. He, on his part, maintained that there never had been anything so far at which to smile in Traffic Division.

Today, he would have held, was no exception.

'Look here, Sloan, I'm ringing from the girl's father's house and there's no way I'm going to let Chummie go until I've charged him.'

'And I,' repeated Sloan, who was Head of the tiny Criminal Investigation Department at Berebury, 'am telling you, Harry, that there is nothing that you can properly charge him with.'

'I'll find something,' growled Inspector Harpe, 'if I have to throw the whole ruddy book at him.'

'If you do,' warned Sloan, more of a veteran of the courts even than Happy Harry, 'you're laying yourself open to being done yourself for false imprisonment and arrest.'

'He's imprisoned, all right,' said Inspector Harpe with a certain amount of satisfaction, 'in the girl's car . . .'

'It doesn't matter where . . .'

'And I'm not letting him out of it until I've charged him,' said Harpe with considerable determination.

'Be it on your own head, then.'

'What I want you to tell me is what the charge should be.' He sounded aggrieved. 'You're crime, aren't you?'

'Yes,' said Sloan, beginning to lose patience with his old friend and colleague. 'I am, Harry, and I'm telling you that you've got no case . . .'

'Listen,' said Inspector Harpe. 'There's this young girl – Julie something – little slip of a thing, doing nursing up at the hospital, on some sort of funny split duty in the evening.'

'Twilight,' supplied Sloan. 'I know.'

'Comes off duty at half eleven, which is bad enough for a girl to be out late like that on her own . . .'

'Where have you been for the last twenty years, Harry? You're out of touch.'

'I don't know what you're talking about.'

'Try telling any girl over the age of consent that she shouldn't be out alone any time she wants to – day or night – and she'll make mincemeat of you, Harry.'

'I reckon this one might change her mind about that now.'

'That's as may be,' said Sloan.

'What happened,' said Harpe, determined to have his say, 'was that when she came off duty she collected her car from the nurses' car park. That's well lit, all right, and there was nobody about except the rest of that shift going off duty at the same time.'

'They used to live in nurses' homes,' said Detective Inspector Sloan, reminiscently, 'with a regular battle-axe as Home Sister. She locked 'em in after work.'

'They were let out for the Police Ball,' said Inspector

Harpe, married man now but bachelor once.

'And we were invited in for the Nurses' one.' Sloan sighed.

There was a slight pause for the happy remembrance of things past and then Inspector Harpe resumed his narrative.

'She gets in her car and starts out for home – she lives with her parents right out in the country the other side of Larking.'

'Quite a drive on your own at night,' observed Sloan. 'Cross-country with a vengeance.'

'Exactly!' Happy Harry seemed obscurely pleased with this remark.

'So?'

'You know Carr's Bottom?'

'Of course I know Carr's Bottom, Harry,' said Sloan with pardonable irritation. 'I may not be in Traffic but I do know my Calleshire roads.'

'Where you come down the hill and there's a bend at the bottom before you get to that little bridge over the water there. Hammon something.'

'Hammon Penne,' supplied Sloan. 'A penne is a managed stream.'

'Just there,' said Harpe tensely. 'Well, this girl Julie comes down the hill on her way home from the hospital, drives over the bridge and then has to stop a bit sharp because she sees there's a big cardboard box in the middle of the road.'

'Which is particularly narrow there?'

'I'll say,' Inspector Harpe endorsed this warmly. 'Too narrow for her to get past anyway. She can see the box is empty and reckons it's fallen off the back of a lorry . . .'

'Quite a few things do,' said Sloan with quiet irony.

'What's that? Oh, yes, of course . . .' Happy Harry acknowledged this and hurried on. 'Well, naturally the girl gets out of her car and goes to shift the obstruction out of her way.'

'Naturally,' said Detective Inspector Sloan drily.

'No problem there. It's quite lightweight and she lifts it off the road and goes and gets back into her car.' Harpe paused impressively. 'That's when her troubles began.'

'Tell me,' said Sloan unnecessarily.

'While she's been doing all this another car – a big one – comes down the road behind her and slows down. She starts off as quickly as she can because of course he can't overtake her on account of the road being so narrow there.'

'No.'

'The trouble was, she says, not only that he wouldn't dim his headlights but that he drove right up close behind her after she started off.'

Sloan gave it as his opinion that this was always difficult and bad driving into the bargain.

'That's what I would have said first, too,' said Harpe mysteriously. 'So as soon as the road got wide enough for him to overtake she pulled over to the left of the road and slowed down for him to get on with it.'

'And he didn't?' said Sloan, since presumably there wouldn't have been any story if he had.

'Too right, he didn't. He just clung to her tail. The girl – I said she was called Julie something, didn't I? – started to get more than a bit worried then.'

'I don't blame her,' said Detective Inspector Sloan, who had seen quite enough bodies of girls in ditches in his time.

'And when he followed her when she turned off the Carr's Bottom road down the long lane along the valley towards Almstone – you know, Seedy, where the wood comes right to the edge of the road . . .'

'I know. Hammon Lane . . .'

'. . . she began to be really scared.'

'Yes,' said Sloan moderately. 'I can see that she might.'

'As you know there aren't any houses along that road that she could have pulled into for help – especially at that hour of the night.'

'It is lonely there,' conceded Sloan.

'But there was nothing she could do to shake him off or get him to put his lights off. She went fast and she went slow and she flashed her own lights on and off . . .'

'But he didn't take the hint?'

'You could put it like that.'

'So?'

'She tossed up between trying to drive right into the middle of Berebury into the Police Station yard . . .'

'She might just have found somewhere to park there,' observed Sloan bitterly, 'seeing it was practically the middle of the night, but I wouldn't have counted on it myself.'

'. . . or driving straight home, which was in fact by this time a lot nearer.'

As the police professional in Calleshire most involved with murder, Detective Inspector Sloan would have been the last man in the world to subscribe to the view that 'East or West, Home's Best' since home was where most victims of murder met their end. This instance, he was prepared to concede, might just be the exception that proved the rule.

'Be it ever so humble,' he said, 'there's no place like home.'

'She knew her father would be in, you see,' said Harpe. 'So . . .'

'So she made for Larking as fast as she could.'

'Other driver still in hot pursuit?'

'Right behind her,' said Harpe. 'Headlights still turned up and he wouldn't be shaken off, no matter what she did.'

'Alarming,' agreed Sloan.

'I'll say,' Harry Harpe endorsed this vigorously. 'Anyway, she gets to Larking and turns into her own entrance and blow me, this chap turns in, too, and pulls up right behind her . . .'

'Headlights still on?' said Sloan.

'Full. The girl leaps out of her car, locks the door and dashes inside, shouting for her father.'

'What does the other driver do?'

'Nothing at all,' said Harpe impressively. 'Just stays in his vehicle.'

'Funny, that,' mused Sloan.

'Exactly!' said Harpe triumphantly. 'Now, listen to this. The father comes straight out of the house breathing fire. He goes up to the chap in the car . . .'

'Who hasn't moved and who hasn't switched his head-lights off . . .'

'Right! The father stands by the driver's door and asks him to kindly tell him what he thinks he's doing, or words to that effect . . .'

'Yes?'

'Blow me the chap isn't fazed at all. Says that before he blows his top would the father like to take a look on the floor in front of the back seat of his daughter's car and, by the way, not to unlock the car door until he's sent for the police.'

'Chummie?'

'Crouched on the floor, trying to keep his head down out of the light,' said Inspector Harpe. 'He'd been hiding in the ditch beside the bridge at Carr's Bottom when the girl stopped her car to lift the cardboard carton out of her way.'

'Which Chummie'd put there in the first place,' contributed Sloan.

'The car driver behind saw him climb in and Julie get

back into the car without being aware that he was there inside.'

'Tricky for him,' said Sloan.

'He did a bit of quick thinking and reckoned that if he kept his headlights on Chummie wouldn't dare lift his head above the skyline or harm the girl – not all the while he knew the other chap had spotted him.'

'And if he'd stopped to ring us,' said Sloan realistically, 'there would have been no knowing where Chummie and the girl might have got to by the time we found them.'

'Or in what state she would have been in,' said Harpe. 'Nice girl,' the Traffic man added irrelevantly.

Detective Inspector Sloan scratched his chin. 'I still don't see what you're going to charge him with, Harry.'

'Something,' said Harry flatly.

'He wasn't carrying any scarf or piece of string, was he?'

'Don't know yet,' said Harpe. 'He's still inside the car with one of my constables keeping an eye. Why?'

'If he'd been carrying it with a view to garrotting her, then you might get away with charging him with carrying an offensive weapon but on the other hand, you might not.'

'It's worth a try, seeing as you can garrotte anyone with almost anything.'

'And you can be charged with fitting up more easily than you might like, Harry.'

'I'm not letting him go.'

'I don't know that you'd get away with a charge of criminal intentions either,' said Sloan. 'Some clever dick could argue that he'd been offered a lift by the girl. The other driver doesn't come on the scene, remember, until Chummie is actually clambering out of the ditch and into the car.'

'I don't care what I do him for,' said Inspector Harpe with an admirable devotion to justice and a reprehensible lack of concern for the letter of the law, 'but I'm going to do him for something even if it's only civil trespass or even Breach of the Peace. I should have thought it was conduct liable to put a citizen into a state of fear or alarm.'

Detective Inspector Sloan thought for a long moment. 'The only thing I can think of, Harry—' he began, but he was interrupted.

'I just want him in court. I don't mind what for. When the Press hear the whole story, they'll make his life a misery for the rest of time. And,' he added righteously, 'it might save some other young thing from a fate worse than death.'

'Listen. Take his fingerprints, and get those on the cardboard box, and if they match then charge him under one of the oldest Statutes of the Realm.'

'Which one?' asked Harry suspiciously.

'Wilful obstruction of the Queen's Highway,' said Sloan, adding gently, 'You should have thought of that, Harry. You're Traffic, aren't you?'

Double Jeopardy

'COME ALONG IN and sit down, Sloan,' commanded Dr Dabbe, 'and save your legs.'

'Yes, doctor,' said Detective Inspector Sloan. He was anxious to collect an urgent report from the pathologist.

'Varicose veins are an occupational hazard in the police force, you know.'

'Thank you, doctor.' Detective Inspector Sloan accepted the pathologist's invitation with alacrity, although no one could have described the office attached to the hospital mortuary as exactly cosy.

'That report you're waiting for'll be along in a minute. My secretary's doing you a copy now.'

'Never stand when you can sit,' observed Detective Constable Crosby sententiously from somewhere near the door. 'And never sit when you can lie down.'

'You can lie down if you like, Crosby,' offered the pathologist. He jerked his shoulder in the direction of the mortuary door. 'Plenty of slabs next door. All empty except one – there's an old chap on that who's died from a very old disease. I shouldn't share with him if I were you.'

'No, thank you!' said the Detective Constable with vigour.

'A very old disease,' mused the pathologist. 'I've been wondering what they treated him with.'

'If he's on your mortuary table,' remarked Detective

Inspector Sloan logically, 'whatever treatment he had doesn't seem to have done him all that much good.'

'In my father's day,' said Dr Dabbe reminiscently, 'there was an old and dangerous treatment to go with this old and dangerous disease.'

'Fair enough,' said Sloan, since it sounded to him very like a case of Hamlet's 'Diseases desperate grown by desperate appliance are reliev'd, or not at all.' He said so to Dr Dabbe.

'More like "His dissolute disease will scarce obey this medicine",' said Dr Dabbe. He winked. 'I've always thought *The Merry Wives of Windsor* knew a thing or two.'

'Like that, is it?' said Detective Inspector Sloan.

'The medical treatment – therapy was not a word then in such common use – for gonorrhoea,' carried on Dabbe, 'was to give the patient a high fever.'

'A hair of the dog that bit you?' enquired Detective Constable Crosby insouciantly.

'The deliberate infection of the sufferer with the disease caused by *Plasmodium falciparum* malaria,' said Dr Dabbe impressively.

'Well, I never!' said Crosby, whose mother had even had trouble with him when he was vaccinated.

'The rationale was – well, let us say,' amended the pathologist, 'enquiring medical minds had postulated – that the rigors, to say nothing of the rigours, of the malarial infection would destroy the delicate *Niesseria* gonorrhoea organism.'

'And did they?' asked Detective Inspector Sloan, since they had time on their hands.

'I only heard of the one case myself,' said Dr Dabbe, 'and that was from my father, although I did read that someone had recalled in fiction* the causing of a very high

*Klawans, Harold L., *Sins of Commission*, London, Headline Books (1982).

fever therapeutically in those suffering from primary syphilis.'

' "A good book is the precious life-blood of a master spirit",' quoted Crosby, since it had been printed on the inside cover of one of his school-books.

'Yes, well, as it happens, it's life-blood that we're talking about,' said Dabbe, 'and that's always precious. This was in the Second World War. An old mental asylum had been commandeered by the authorities to be used as an acute general hospital.' He spun round suddenly. 'Do you two know what a padded cell is like?'

'I've heard of them,' said Detective Inspector Sloan cautiously. The exigencies of constabulary service had not led him into one as either patient or policeman.

So far.

'We don't have them down at the nick,' said Detective Constable Crosby.

'The padding on the walls of the cell where this particular medical drama was played out,' said the pathologist, 'served two purposes. One was to deaden sound and the other was to stop the patient injuring himself.' He pursed his lips and added, 'Or herself.'

'Quite,' said Sloan, unsure whether this was a blow against Women's Lib or not.

'There's usually a small high window there – out of reach, of course . . .'

'Of course,' chorused the two policemen.

'And barred, too,' said Dabbe, 'leaving just what Oscar Wilde called 'the little tent of blue which prisoners call the sky', which is there to let in light and air but not to let out the patient.'

'And not,' said Sloan fairly, 'to let in the gaze of people outside.'

'You've got the idea, Sloan,' said Dr Dabbe warmly. 'The floor's sometimes of cork tiles to deaden sound . . .'

'Like the house of that French writer who went on and on?' suggested Sloan, who had often wondered how that particular author would have got on doing his writing if he'd had to do it as Sloan had to, down at the unquiet police station.

'Just like Marcel Proust, Sloan,' agreed Dabbe, 'but the main thing about a padded cell is that the door only ever has one handle, and that's always on . . .'

'The outside,' said Sloan for him. Some things were the same down at the police station.

'And it had a Judas window,' the raconteur completed his description.

'What's a Judas window?' asked Crosby.

'A sort of one-way mirror,' said Dabbe.

'Oh, I've heard of them.' Crosby went a bit pink. 'So that the person on the other side doesn't know when there's someone watching.'

'This hospital, doctor . . .' said Sloan.

'When my father was there in the war, it was treating all sorts and conditions of men and disease – including a number of Lascar seamen with gonorrhoea . . . You know what sailors are . . .'

'By giving them malaria?' asked Sloan a trifle repressively.

'That's right, Sloan. And it was the duty of the House Physician to inoculate these patients by means of the only known method . . .'

'Which was?' asked Sloan, hoping to keep the conversation clinical.

'The bite of the anophelene mosquito.' Dr Dabbe chuckled. 'Believe it or not, these mosquitoes were kept captive in the hospital's dispensary . . .'

'Along with the leeches, I suppose,' said Sloan.

'I bet that that was before the Animal Liberationist people had got going,' said Crosby feelingly. He had sus-

tained injuries once at a march in aid of Animal Rights. It
had been at the hands of a group not at all interested in
the protection of the endangered species known as
unarmed police constables.

'And, as I don't need to remind you, gentlemen' – the
pathologist was not interested in either leeches or the
Animal Liberation Movement – 'such mosquitoes are
dangerous.'

'I can see that they would be,' said Sloan, something of
a specialist himself in the dangerous, if not the endangered.

'It was delivered to the ward from the dispensary in a
corked test-tube.' Dr Dabbe had obviously learned nar-
ration skills at his father's knee because he went on: 'The
Lascar seaman was languishing on his bed in the padded
cell and a young nurse accompanied the doctor in a way
that was *de rigueur* in the dear dead days of long ago.'

There was a pause in tribute to yesteryear. Detective
Constable Crosby shuffled his feet and Dr Dabbe smiled.

'This young nurse stood on the left of the bed and was
thus nearest to the door. This is important and you should
remember it.'

'Yes, doctor,' said Sloan patiently.

'The House Physician went round to the other side of
the bed and therefore had the bed between him and the
door,' said Dr Dabbe. 'Well, my fa— this House Physician
removed the cork from the test-tube and applied the open
end of it to the seaman's arm.'

'So . . .' said Crosby, shifting his weight from one foot
to the other.

'So far, so good,' said the pathologist. 'The anophelene
mosquito, which had been kept hungry, applied itself to
the patient's forearm with all the vigour of its kind . . .'

'Being out for blood, in a manner of speaking,' said
Sloan, conscious that Superintendent Leeyes would be out

for his blood if he didn't get back to the police station with that report soon.

'Exactly, Sloan. When it had had its fill, it withdrew its proboscis or whatever.' The pathologist gave a wicked grin. 'That it had also ingested a good dose of cla— well, gonorrhea, troubled the mosquito not at all. This infection,' added Dr Dabbe hortatively, 'sometimes known as the English disease, not being one to which gnats of the genus *Culex* are susceptible.'

'You learn something every day, don't you?' observed Crosby chattily.

Dr Dabbe was not deflected. 'In this respect, as the poet had it, only man is vile.'

'Yes, doctor.' It was a lesson Sloan had learned early on in his police career.

'Well, what this little beast had enjoyed, Sloan, was the heady taste of freedom . . .'

For a moment Sloan was not sure whether the pathologist was talking about the mosquito or the patient.

'. . . and when it came to going back into the test-tube, I'm afraid that the insect wasn't having any of that and escaped.'

'Oh, dear,' said the Detective Inspector, stealing a surreptitious glance at his watch.

'Exactly,' said Dr Dabbe. 'The nurse acted first and with great presence of mind.'

'She got out?' said Crosby.

Dr Dabbe nodded. 'Being nearest to the door, she made for it, shot through it, and then slammed it shut behind her.'

'Good for her,' said Crosby.

'But not good for my fa— the House Physician, Crosby. That left him, the Lascar seaman and the mosquito together in the padded cell, which, best beloved, you will remember had no door handle on the inside.'

' "Best beloved"?' echoed Detective Constable Crosby, mystified.

'Never mind,' said his superior officer. 'Carry on, doctor.'

'Well, the seaman, having the nasty gonorrhoea already, and it was to be hoped, now malaria as well, had nothing to lose and remained calm and disinterested throughout.'

'Good for him,' said Crosby.

'And the mosquito, already a carrier of *Plasmodium falciparum* malaria and now perhaps also of *Neisseria* gonorrhoea too, was, at least, not as hungry as he had been.'

'That was something,' said Sloan.

'For the unhappy House Physician,' said Dr Dabbe, 'growing older by the minute, rather more was at stake. Were he to be bitten by the mosquito he would be at risk of being infected not only by malaria but possibly by the gonococcus, too.'

'And he would know it, too,' said Sloan, 'being medical himself.'

'Not so much a case of a little learning being a dangerous thing,' said Dr Dabbe judiciously, 'as a lot of learning being downright terrifying.'

'What happened next?' asked Crosby in a manner dear to all narrators.

'He started to yell to be let out, of course,' said Dr Dabbe.

'Not unnaturally,' said Sloan, feeling something of a captive listener himself.

'But the nurses on the outside of that locked door yelled back: "Not on your life!" "It is on my life . . ." wailed the poor fellow, urgently trying to remember what he'd learned about malaria and gonorrhoea.'

'Neither prospect exactly pleasing,' said Sloan not unsympathetically.

'Taking several propitiatory oaths about his future conduct,' said Dr Dabbe drily, 'to do with remaining chaste for the rest of his life and never visiting Afric's burning shores, he set about trying to catch the mosquito.'

'Quite so,' said Sloan, stealing another glance at his watch. Time was getting on.

'What happened next?' asked Crosby.

Dr Dabbe chuckled. 'The young ladies outside the door of the padded cell, all wearing the uniform of those dedicated to the selfless care of the sick, chanted: "Kill it, kill it, and then we'll open the door." '

'They would,' said Crosby feelingly.

'It never does to trust someone you can't see though,' pronounced Sloan. 'Never.'

'No,' agreed Dr Dabbe, 'but perhaps it was just as well they didn't trust him because he – deceitful fellow – called out that he had killed it.'

'And he hadn't?' said Crosby, unversed as yet in real cupidity. 'What happened?'

'Ah,' said the pathologist, 'the watch of Nightingales on the other side of the cell-door had heard the siren songs of newly qualified young doctors before and were not deceived. They demanded to be shown the body.'

'Quite right,' said Crosby stoutly.

'The cunning young man countered that he would when they opened the door. "Show us through the Judas window," the nurses trilled sweetly,' recounted the pathologist, showing all the skills of a real tale-spinner. 'One of the nurses whose father was a judge even called out "Habeas Corpus" . . .'

Detective Inspector Sloan gave it as his considered

opinion that invoking the law was seldom helpful in a real emergency.

'Then,' said Dabbe histrionically, 'the House Physician suddenly went quiet.'

'Saying his prayers, was he?' asked Sloan.

'The hapless fellow had been struck by a horrid thought,' said Dabbe. 'He'd just remembered that the tsetse fly – *Glossina morsitans* – which is the vector of sleeping sickness – African trypanosomiasis – is led to its victims by the odour of their breath. Mind you, gentlemen, he was pretty flustered and not yet sufficiently sophisticated to think it through . . .'

It crossed Detective Inspector Sloan's mind that the time would probably come when forensic scientists would be able to track down criminals in the same way.

Dr Dabbe was talking about the past not the future. 'The House Physician said afterwards that he wasn't taking any chances with the anophelene mosquito.'

'Quite right,' said Sloan.

'So he shut his mouth and kept it shut while he sought a weapon.'

'Quite right,' said Sloan again. It was a course of action he approved on principle.

'Only, of course, there wasn't a weapon immediately at hand. Not in an old padded cell.'

'No.'

'So it came about,' said the pathologist, 'that those looking through the Judas window were treated to the engaging spectacle of a white-coated young doctor in hot pursuit of a mercifully replete mosquito round a padded cell, brandishing a small pocket *vade mecum* of pharmacology, *circa* 1941, published in conformity with war-time economy standards.'

'And,' enquired Sloan, his glance straying back to his watch, 'was the race to the swift?'

'Well,' replied Dr Dabbe judiciously, 'the House Physician was no match for the mosquito at ducking and diving although he was quite good on the Rugby field. The hospital, you understand, had been in need of a wing three-quarter at the time of his admission.'

'Oh, I understand all right,' said Sloan.

'The contest was in some respects – especially to those who witnessed it – reminiscent of that between Sancho Panza and the windmill . . .'

'Was he a boxer?' asked Crosby suspiciously.

'No, Crosby, he wasn't,' said Dr Dabbe, 'but it doesn't matter because in the end *Homo sapiens* beat *Culex*, the law of the jungle prevailing.'

'It usually does,' said Sloan.

'Kill or be killed,' said Crosby sententiously.

Dr Dabbe hadn't finished. 'Picking up the dead body of the mosquito, the House Physician waved it triumphantly in front of the Judas window, demanding of the nurses to be let out of the padded cell at last.'

'And?' said Sloan. Surely that report they were waiting for should be ready by now? They were late enough already.

'And,' said Dr Dabbe, 'the door was indeed opened unto him.'

'Good,' said Crosby.

'But,' sighed the pathologist, 'how was he to know that while he had been concentrating on the kill his audience had been swelled – and silenced – by the arrival of a pre-war, pre-Salmon Ward Sister of the old school?'

'How indeed?' said Sloan politely.

'One with a Crimean cast of mind, too . . .' The door of the pathologist's room opened and his secretary appeared with something in her hand but he carried on regardless: 'The poor fellow fell out of the cell and said, "Talk about being clapped out . . ." That was before he realized she was there, of course.' Dabbe paused and said with a touch of melancholy, 'He never made consultant, you know. Had to go into general practice . . .'

Lord Peter's Touch

'HE SAID WHAT?' exploded Superintendent Leeyes irately.

'That the bell-ringers in Almstone church take their names from the characters in a book by Dorothy L. Sayers called *The Nine Tailors* when they're ringing. All eight of them.'

'Do they, indeed!' snorted Leeyes.

Detective Inspector Sloan consulted a list. 'Joe Hinkins, Hezekiah Lavender, Harry Gotobed—'

'You're not having me on, Sloan, are you?' Leeyes interrupted dangerously. 'Because if you are . . .'

'No, sir,' Sloan assured him, resuming his notebook. 'I'm dead serious . . . Jack Godfrey, Esra Wilderspin, Donnington . . .'

'Didn't Donnington have a Christian name, then?'

'Not that the author told us,' said Sloan precisely, 'any more than did Young Pratt . . . No, I'm wrong there, sir. Sorry. My mistake. He was Wally.'

'Are you quite sure that you're not having me on?'

'Quite sure,' said Sloan.

'Anyway, that's only seven,' said the Superintendent, who invariably argued that good detection was always based on minute attention to detail.

'I'm afraid,' sighed Sloan, 'that that's the whole point.'

'Is it?' asked the Superintendent testily. 'Then I'd be obliged if you'd tell me more. I've been waiting to know what the whole point is.'

Detective Inspector Sloan took a deep breath. 'In this book that they're all going on about . . .'

'*The Nine Tailors.* I'd got that far.'

'The eighth ringer, one William Thoday, was taken ill and Lord Peter Wimsey stepped into his shoes.'

'Ah,' said the Superintendent alertly.

'This group of ringers – groups call themselves "towers" by the way . . .'

'Well, it's better than calling themselves "Happy Bands of Pilgrims",' said Leeyes realistically.

'They meet about twice a week to practise and to ring these peals.' Sloan paused and then said, 'Silly, really, I suppose, sir, them taking names like that.'

'It's been done before,' said his superior officer perversely. 'In fiction, anyway.'

'Sir?'

'By Rudyard Kipling in a short story called "The Janeites".' The Superintendent was a great one for attending Adult Education Classes and 'Rudyard Kipling – The Writer and The Man' had been the most recent. 'The people in that were all from Jane Austen's *Emma.*'

'Just like that,' said Sloan, blessing Kipling. As a working policeman the line of that writer's which he liked best was the one describing the crimes of Clapham as being chaste in Martapan but he got straight down to business. 'Last night in Almstone Tower the man on number two bell, William Thoday, couldn't come and a friend of the Rector's stood in for him . . .'

'And?'

'The man on number six bell, who called himself Donnington, got killed.'

43

'By accident? You don't get a lot of accidents bell-ringing, Sloan.'*

'You might say, sir, that he was taken up by excess rope.'

'You might,' responded Leeyes briskly. 'I wouldn't. Put it in plain English.'

'The bell fell over the balance point, Donnington hung on to the rope and went up with it at about fifty miles an hour, hit his head on the beam and fell fifteen feet back on to the stone floor of the bell tower.'

'A Dead Ringer,' commented Leeyes, more of an Edgar Wallace man himself in spite of the classes on Rudyard Kipling.

'They call it a "high-speed lift" among themselves, do the bell-ringers,' said Sloan. 'It's one of the big bells, you see, sir. It must weigh the best part of a thousand kilograms.'

'And how much is that?' The Superintendent would never have any truck with measurements devised by Napoleon Bonaparte.

'Well over nineteen hundredweight.' Sloan paused. 'This visitor of the Rector's seemed to know what he was doing, though. After he'd made sure that there was nothing to be done for this man Donnington he went up into the belfry to have a looksee . . .'

'Couldn't wait for us to get there, I suppose,' grumbled the Superintendent. 'That's the worst of amateurs.'

'When he got up there,' continued Sloan, 'he found that the stay was broken. The stay, sir, is what supports the bell.'

---

*The Superintendent was wrong (and not for the first time). See: 1. *British Medical Journal* Volume 301, 22–29 December 1990, pp. 1415–1418: 'Bellringers' bruises and broken bones: capers and crises in campanology' by A. C. Lamont, N. J. M. London. 2. Correspondence. Bellringers' bruises and broken bones. *BMJ* 1991; 302: 291–2. 3. Ditto *BMJ* 303: 1553.

'I could work that out for myself, thank you, Sloan,' said Leeyes. 'Why did the stay break?'

'The wood was rotten with woodworm,' said Sloan.

'Don't they inspect it?' asked Leeyes, 'And treat it?'

'Yes to both those things, sir. But that wasn't what this friend of the Rector's wanted to know.'

'All right then, tell me. I suppose I'm never too old to learn.'

There would have been nobody at the police station at Berebury who subscribed to this view of the Superintendent, but all Sloan said was: 'He asked if the man calling himself Donnington always took that bell.'

'And did he?'

'Yes, sir. Though it's not usual these days to stick to the same bell.' It wasn't usual not to have any women either but Sloan didn't say so. This was no moment for feminism. He hurried on. 'Then I'm told this chap – I did say he was a gentleman, didn't I, sir? – took out a rather old-fashioned sort of eyeglass and had a good look at the bolts keeping the stays in but talking nonsense all the while he did it. "Fop first, hero second" was how Jack Godfrey described him to me afterwards.'

'If you ask me,' said Leeyes gratuitously, 'it sounds as if they had had the vapid Sir Percy Blakeney with them.'

' "The Scarlet Pimpernel"?' Sloan must have been all of eleven years old when he'd first read that book. 'Oh, no, sir, I don't think so. Not,' he added hastily, 'that we're not all literary inheritors in our way.' As far as the Calleshire force was concerned, opinion on the Superintendent's origins was divided between two schools of thought: Ghenghis Khan and Harold Hardaxe.

Leeyes grunted. 'That's as may be. How much evidence had this character destroyed by the time you got there?'

'None, sir. On the contrary. He wouldn't let anyone at

all into the bell-chamber until our people arrived.'

'That's something, I suppose,' said Leeyes grudgingly. 'Then what?'

'He said we should treat it as a case of murder and then he went off to talk to the Rector.'

'Leaving us to hold the baby . . .'

'Not quite, sir. He came back about ten minutes later with the reverend gentleman and said we should arrest the man going under the name of Wilderspin. Seems as if in real life he's a carpenter.'

'That doesn't make him a murderer.'

'No, sir, but he's the one among them who best knows about wood.'

'What about it?'

'This friend of the Rector's said that all the wood in the church tower was chestnut except for the bell-stay. Chestnut doesn't rot – or at least hardly at all – especially in the dry.'

'So?'

'This bell stay was pitchpine.'

'Well?'

'Bell stays are always made of ash.'

'Are you going to come to the point while I'm still on duty, Sloan?'

'Pitchpine, which is highly subject to woodworm into the bargain, wouldn't hold. It hasn't got the spring of ash. This chap – the visitor – said it must have been put there with malice aforethought and was there any reason for anyone wanting to kill Donnington.'

'And was there?'

'Oh, yes. He'd been carrying on with Wilderspin's wife.'

'Sloan, what did the Rector call this friend of his?'

'*Sui generis.*'

Memory Corner

'HE SAID WHAT?' echoed Detective Inspector Sloan in disbelief.

'Would we kindly step round,' repeated Detective Constable Crosby, 'when we had a moment, because he'd just killed a man.'

Sloan groaned. 'A nutter?'

'To Almstone College at the University.'

'An academic nutter, then?'

'I don't know, sir,' said Detective Constable Crosby. 'That's all he said.'

'And who, might I ask, is he?'

Detective Constable Crosby glanced down at his notebook. 'Edward Francis Mainprice Linthwaite. He made me write it all down and read it back to him. Very particular about it, he was.'

'H'm.'

'Most murderers don't bother about the spelling of their names, do they, sir? And the exact time,' said Crosby. 'He made me write that down, too, sir. He said he always understood that in these matters time was' – the Constable frowned at the effort of recollection – 'time was of the essence.'

'Sounds to me,' said Sloan resignedly, 'as if what he needs are two little men in white coats, not a pair of heavily overworked detectives. All right, Crosby. Let's go.'

This baleful view was reinforced by the total calm prevailing in the Porter's Lodge at Almstone College. Enquiries for an Edward Linthwaite produced a response in which lay the gentlest of reproofs. 'The Professor of Twentieth-Century English Literature, gentlemen,' said the porter, 'has his rooms in the main quadrangle.'

Sloan, who at another time might have wondered aloud whether there was any such thing at all as a literature of the twentieth century, followed the porter's pointing finger with his eye.

'See – over there on your right – the first-floor rooms with the bay window,' said the porter, who, having no great faith in the Force, added: 'You can't miss the quadrangle archway.'

'On your mark, Crosby,' said Sloan in quite a different tone of voice. 'Get set. Go.'

The door to Professor Linthwaite's rooms was opened to them by a short spare man, who looked worried.

'If that's the police, Arthur,' called out a deep voice from behind him, 'let them in.'

'It is,' said Sloan.

'Good, good,' boomed the voice, its owner still unseen. 'No point in hanging about at this stage, is there?' There was a movement inside the room and a stout, untidily dressed figure hove into view. 'Besides, his people will have to be told as soon as possible, won't they?'

The college room was a very beautiful one, the walls panelled in oak and lined with books. Its largest piece of furniture was a great Knole sofa facing the fireplace. It was tastefully upholstered in a material and design that owed more than something to the great medieval tapestry workshops of the Low Countries. What was less appealing was the body of a young man lying on it with much of his head covered in blood.

On an elegant sofa-table set behind this piece of furniture

lay – on top of an academic journal – a blood-stained poker. On the floor, almost hidden by the frill of the sofa, was a lady's handbag.

'I'm sorry about the mess,' said the stout man, as if reading Sloan's thoughts. 'I've never killed a man before.' He seemed to collect himself. 'Oh, I'm sorry. This is Professor Arthur Maple, who is Calle Professor of Moral Law here at the University. He happened to come round just – er – afterwards.'

'And you are . . . ?' said Sloan, concentrating on the stout figure. He was wearing a flowery-patterned shirt without a tie. There was something odd about his shirt, but Sloan wasn't sure quite what.

'Professor Linthwaite, Inspector. Edward Francis . . .'

'Mainprice Linthwaite,' finished Detective Constable Crosby for him.

'And who,' enquired Sloan frostily, 'is the dead man?' The edge of the coloured silk shirt was peeping out untidily from under one of the professor's cuffs.

'Good question,' said Linthwaite as one encouraging a backward pupil.

'You don't know?' asked Crosby in spite of himself.

'I know his surname naturally, officer. It's Carstairs. But not his Christian names.' Linthwaite waved a hand. 'The Dean will know, though, won't he, Arthur? The Dean's very good about that sort of thing – besides, he'll have a list. Bound to.'

'So the dead man is a student here,' said Sloan, half-expecting the Mad Hatter to drop in at any minute to join the throng. Or perhaps, in view of the handbag, Mrs Linthwaite. If there was a Mrs Linthwaite. He was beginning to doubt it.

'Oh, yes, Inspector.' Linthwaite looked surprised. 'That's the whole trouble. Didn't you know?'

'Not quite the whole trouble,' said Sloan with a touch

of acerbity. 'Suppose you start at the beginning . . .'

Linthwaite beamed. 'Good, good. Primary sources are so important . . . I always tell my students to go back to first things.'

'Edward,' warned Professor Maple, 'this is not a lecture.' He glanced at the body of the dead man and then averted his eyes. 'Nor even a demonstration.'

'I know that,' said the stout man indignantly. 'Well, the whole business began, Inspector, at the beginning of the academic year when a University Senate Sub-Committee decided to institute a series of inter-disciplinary lectures and meetings.'

'Leading, it was hoped,' augmented Arthur Maple, rolling his eyes heavenwards, 'to some cross-faculty thinking.'

Detective Constable Crosby, who had had to have cross-dressing explained to him very carefully indeed, looked totally bewildered.

'Not, though, surely,' said Detective Inspector Sloan with some irritation, 'Professor Linthwaite, leading to a dead man on your sofa.'

'Oh, yes it did,' retorted Professor Linthwaite vigorously. 'You see, these lectures were designed to bring scientists and artsmen together. The theory – decussation, it might well be called – was that nuclear physicists should know about Wittgenstein and so forth . . .'

'Edward,' warned Professor Maple, 'I think you should leave Wittgenstein out of this.'

'Not a help?'

Arthur Maple shook his head. 'No.'

'Oh, all right, if you say so. I can't leave Darwin out, though, because he comes into things.'

There were those down at the Police Station, thought Sloan, who would agree with that. They had no quarrel at all with the Darwinian view of the origin of the species.

Especially on Saturday evenings after a home football match.

'He comes into the evolution side – with Lamarck, of course,' puffed Linthwaite. 'Well, I gave the lectures myself. On Orwell and Huxley, mostly . . .'

'And this man Carstairs was in the audience?' hazarded Sloan.

'So he said.' Professor Linthwaite nodded. 'That was when he came to see me afterwards. He was a human biologist.'

'Ah,' said Sloan. Carstairs didn't look like a human anything any more: just a very dead young man. 'What did he come to see you about?'

'Something I'd said in my lectures.'

'About Orwell and Huxley or Darwin?' Sloan had never even heard of Lamarck.

'Huxley. Only being a scientist he'd got the wrong Huxley, of course.'

'There were two?'

'Three actually, Thomas Henry and Julian, who were biologists, and Aldous who was the author of a famous work called *Brave New World*.'

'So . . .'

'In that book,' explained Professor Linthwaite, 'Aldous Huxley had postulated a future state in which it would be possible to program people's minds to think in a particular way . . .'

'I see.'

'And George Orwell had gone a bit further than that in his works by hypothesizing the Thought Police from whom – if I might paraphrase the Collect for Purity – no secrets are hid . . .'

'And?' Detective Inspector Sloan would have been the first to say that although he knew nothing about twentieth-century English literature he did know whom he liked. It was therefore a couple of chilling lines from a poem by Rudyard Kipling which then came into his own mind:

> There is neither Evil nor Good in life
> Except as the needs of the State ordain.

'. . . and,' went on Linthwaite hortatively, 'as you probably know, the Thought Police were there to check on possible subversion before it happened.'

Detective Constable Crosby's head had come up at the first mention of the word 'police' but he still looked puzzled.

'I was really lecturing,' said the Professor, 'on the great divide between the literature of the past and what writers – not scientists – imagine will be discovered in the future . . .'

Sloan looked down at his notebook and then at the body. It was a quite different – but infinitely greater – divide that young Carstairs had already crossed: thanks entirely, apparently, to Professor Linthwaite.

'Should,' enquired the Detective Inspector, 'your lecture have been so very – er – upsetting, then?' He'd just worked out what was odd about the man's shirt. It was the buttons.

Sloan got an oblique response.

'I understand, Inspector, that Carstairs was a particularly gifted student in his own field.' Linthwaite turned to Professor Maple. 'Is that not so, Arthur?'

'He was a quite outstanding human biologist,' concurred Arthur Maple at once. 'Undoubtedly Nobel Prize material of the future – although,' he added cautiously, 'I must say you can never be absolutely sure with the Nobel Prize Committee these days.'

Sloan, whose own view was that no sensible man could always be sure of any committee ever, said: 'So Carstairs was gifted . . .'

'In my lecture,' said Linthwaite, 'I'd spoken of memory and how there must be an anatomical or physiological basis for it even if science hadn't yet discovered a way of reading it. The nature of consciousness has always been very much thought about – William Shakespeare, for instance, put memory in the *pia mater* of the brain. Well,' he paused impressively, 'Carstairs went away and found it.'

'Just like that?'

'Just like that, Inspector. He came up with the answer to the Chinese philosopher Lao Tse's famous question, "How can you know what I know?" '

'So you killed him?' interjected Crosby in the tones of one anxious to get everything absolutely clear.

Professor Linthwaite might not have been accustomed to murder but he knew all about enquiring young men to whom matters had to be explained. He turned to Crosby. 'I gave him what the poet called "the lead gift in the twilight",' he said patiently, 'because it wouldn't have done for men to be able to read other men's memories. Never.'

Detective Inspector Sloan turned over a fresh page of his notebook and let the Professor carry on. The groves of academe were obviously as sinister as all the other groves he had ever known: including the old oak ones at the edge of Berebury Common.

'You see,' carried on the Professor, 'Carstairs went home after my lecture and did a lot of thinking and then set up some experiments on his own account.'

Sloan could see, all right. Now.

'The memory cells,' said Linthwaite, every bit as didactic in his own way as Superintendent Leeyes down at the Police Station, 'must be there or none of us would be able to remember anything. Right?'

'Right,' responded Crosby, clearly fascinated.

'Well, Carstairs therefore reasoned that what was needed

was merely a way of getting at those cells and then reading them . . .'

'Easy if you say it quickly,' said Crosby.

'Then, gentlemen, when he'd demonstrated that he'd discovered how to see into the human memory, he came to see me. It was all in the cells, he said, but I can't say exactly which cells because I'm not a scientist.'

'You are a murderer, though,' pointed out Sloan, with quite a different sort of cell in mind.

'My goodness, yes,' acknowledged Professor Linthwaite readily. 'It seemed the only course of action open to me when Carstairs told me that from now on it would be possible for everyone's memory to be read as easily as if it were a cinematograph film . . .'

'Did he attempt to prove it to you?' asked Sloan curious to know what Linthwaite would say.

'Not only did he try, but he succeeded,' said Linthwaite, shuffling his feet and looking disconcerted for the first time. 'And very unnerving it was, too. Told me exactly what I thought about the Master of Almstone.'

'That's hardly a secret,' said Arthur Maple acidly.

'But that means,' blurted out Crosby, 'that we wouldn't need oaths or juries . . .'

'Or examinations either,' said Linthwaite, ever the dominie.

'It would be the lie detector to end all lie detectors, too,' said Sloan thoughtfully.

Arthur Maple, Professor of Moral Law, coughed. 'Actually, gentlemen, if you consider it for a moment, I think you will agree it would be the end of all investigative and judicial processes as we know them now.'

'Make politics a bit difficult, too, wouldn't it?' said Crosby cheerfully.

'More than that. Society would run the risk of breaking

down entirely,' insisted Linthwaite warmly. 'There was an essay of G. K. Chesterton's in which everyone had had to tell the truth.' He shook his head. 'Led to some pretty nasty situations, I can tell you. And that was only fiction.'

'And Carstairs had told nobody of this discovery of his?' barked Sloan, light dawning as he took another look at Linthwaite's shirt.

'Nobody. He assured me of that. He said he wanted me to be the first to know, before he sent anything off for publication.' Linthwaite frowned. 'But I'm afraid he wasn't prepared to see the terrible implications of what he had established.'

That, thought Sloan to himself, hadn't stopped Alfred Nobel's work on dynamite either.

Crosby muttered: 'They wouldn't ever need psychologists or psychiatrists, either, would they? They'd know what was going on in a man's mind anyway without asking.'

Detective Inspector Sloan ignored the tempting luxury of considering a world without trick-cyclists. 'You tried to reason with him, I take it?' he said to the professor. 'After you'd realized the profound implications of what Carstairs had found out?'

'I did indeed but he was very arrogant,' said Linthwaite. 'He wasn't interested in the dangers of a destabilized society at all. He insisted instead that all knowledge was ultimately valuable to humanity and should be available to all researchers on principle.'

They had Records Officers in the Calleshire County Constabulary Headquarters – and no doubt in government offices, too – who thought along similar lines . . . power lines.

'It's a great pity that young Carstairs wasn't less like Galileo Galilei and more like Copernicus,' remarked Professor Maple, still not looking at the sofa.

'Sir?' Sloan looked in his direction.

'Galileo announced his discoveries about the force of gravity to the world,' the Professor of Moral Law informed him, 'and got hauled up in front of the Inquisition for his pains. Copernicus only let them find out he was right about the earth going round the sun after he'd died.'

'Much safer,' agreed Sloan shortly. He was thinking about something curious that was more local.

'And Arthur here,' persisted Linthwaite, 'agreed with me that most human beings would find it intolerable for other people to have access to their innermost thoughts and rec-ollections.'

Professor Maple said hastily, as if expecting to be charged as an accessory after the fact, 'I dare say in the fullness of time – several generations, perhaps – the human race would accustom itself to the new situation but to begin with . . .'

'Bargaining would be difficult,' Crosby observed to nobody in particular, 'wouldn't it? I mean, you'd know to start with exactly how far someone was prepared to go before you started.'

'Blackmail,' said Sloan tersely, ignoring the implications of a disintegrated commercial world as not his problem. Crime was.

'Er . . . precisely,' said Maple.

Linthwaite said nothing.

'What we might call Carstairs' working papers . . .' Sloan began aloud.

Professor Linthwaite's gaze turned way from the two policemen and in the direction of the fireplace. Fragments of very burnt paper – sere and friable – fluttered about in the old-fashioned open fire. 'I had to use the poker to get the fire going after I'd killed him but I put it straight back on the table as soon as it had cooled.' He looked quizzically at the policemen. 'You'll be wanting that, won't you?'

The police were going to want a great deal more than the poker but Sloan did not say so. Instead he said formally that they would be taking the Professor in for further questioning in connection with the death of young Carstairs, Christian name unknown.

'Of course,' said Linthwaite readily. 'Arthur will see to things.' He turned. 'Won't you, Arthur? I've a book in the press, you see, and there'll be proofs coming from the printers and so forth . . .'

Detective Inspector said nothing but he had to admire the man's quick thinking. Already in his mind's eye he could see and hear the special pleading of Counsel for the Defence . . . 'Not so much diminished responsibility, members of the jury, but more an enhanced responsibility for society as befits the distinguished academic who stands before you now . . . acting, as he perceived, in the best interests of humanity . . . who shall say how any one of us would have – should have – acted in the same daunting circumstances in which he found himself?'

It, decided Sloan, then and there, wouldn't do.

No one was going to get away with that in his manor.

Linthwaite turned to Sloan with a guileless expression and said, 'You'll want me to come with you now, Inspector, won't you?'

'We will.'

He fingered his open shirt and pointed to a door on the far side of the room. 'I'll just put a tie on and get a few things together. I won't keep you waiting.'

'No,' said Sloan flatly. 'You'll come with us just as you are.'

'No?' He looked surprised and a little pained. 'I thought, Inspector, you could wear your own clothes on remand.'

'You can wear whatever you like,' said Sloan, adding meaningfully, 'as you did this afternoon. But you're not going to change your clothes until we've had a proper look at them.'

Linthwaite started to sweat a little.

'You murdered Carstairs,' said Sloan, 'because he'd discovered something all right, but it wasn't the secret of memory. He surprised you in the clothes of your choice, didn't he? Forget to lock your door, did you?'

The man sank into a chair.

'And he threatened you with exposure as a transvestite unless you paid him Danegeld.' Nobody, thought Sloan, had summed up blackmail better than Rudyard Kipling.

Linthwaite, in spite of his size, seemed suddenly diminished.

'You were taken by surprise and killed him in a fit of unpremeditated anger,' said Sloan inexorably, 'and then before you could quite change back into your other clothes Professor Maple arrived and you had to send for us and cook up this cock-and-bull story about a scientific discovery.' Sloan pointed to Linthwaite's neck, where he had made a discovery on his own part. 'You put a jacket on but you hadn't time to put on a shirt . . .'

Linthwaite put a hand to his throat.

'What you are wearing,' said Sloan, 'buttons up the wrong way round. I think we shall find that that's not a shirt at all but a woman's dress you've got on under there . . .'

Slight of Hand

THE PREMISES of the Mordaunt Club were situated in one of the quieter streets of London's district of St James's. It was thus easily accessible from the higher reaches of Whitehall (in both senses), the Admiralty, the headquarters of certain famous regiments and New – or rather New, New – Scotland Yard.

Membership of the club was open to all those of a similar cast of mind to Sir John Mordaunt, fifth baronet (1650–1721), except for active politicians of any – or, indeed, of no – party. This is because Sir John, although an assiduous Member of Parliament himself in his day, had promised to vote in the House according to the promptings of reason and good sense; in the 'publick good' rather than with selfish 'interest' as it had been put in the early day equivalent of an election address.

Henry Tyler was wont to drift in to have luncheon at the Mordaunt Club at least once a week. Whilst it was perfectly possible to reserve a table there when hosting guests or even when dining unaccompanied it was the happy custom of the club that members themselves, if lunching alone, joined those eating at the long refectory table at the far end of the panelled dining-room.

This was how it was that Henry Tyler came to be sitting next to Commander Alan Howkins, a senior policeman with much on his mind. It was a Monday morning and they were so far alone at the communal luncheon table.

'Good weekend?' enquired Henry Tyler politely. He was a little stiff himself from an excess of gardening at his home in the country and he was glad that the week ahead back at his desk at the Foreign Office promised to be less taxing – physically, at least.

The Commander shook his head. 'Rather disappointing, actually.'

'Sorry about that.'

'Can't expect to win them all, I suppose,' said the policeman.

'True,' observed Henry, projecting the proper sympathy due from a member of one of Her Majesty's Offices of State to another. Lessons about not always winning had been learned at the Foreign and Commonwealth Office a long time ago and had been regularly reinforced by international events over the years.

'But I don't like being beaten,' said Howkins with unexpected savagery.

'Who does?' said Tyler. Not that the Foreign Office ever admitted to being beaten – something which, quite typically there, they saw as completely different from 'not winning'. What they did when it happened – for instance, in 1776 – was to use another expression altogether. The Foreign Office was great on euphemisms.

'Outwitted,' said Howkins, tearing a bread roll apart with unnecessary vigour. 'That's what we were.'

'Ah,' said Tyler. So Scotland Yard, then, didn't go in for euphemisms . . .

'Lost Mr Big,' said Howkins briefly, turning to the hovering waiter. 'I'll have the whitebait, please, and the beef. Under-done.'

'Tough,' said Henry Tyler. 'No, no,' he said hastily to the waiter, 'I wasn't talking about the beef. I'll have that, too.'

(The letters between Sir John Mordaunt and his wife had frequently dwelt on game, brawn, pickled bacon and such-like country fare and a tradition of good cooking was maintained at the club.)

'I suppose it's always the big fish that get away,' resumed the policeman, more philosophically.

'No,' said Henry kindly, 'but you miss them more than the little ones when you do lose them and you remember them for longer.'

'True.'

'Better luck next time, anyway,' said the Foreign Office man.

'That's what the Assistant Commissioner said after the first time,' said Howkins.

'Like that, is it?'

'And after the second time,' murmured the Commander into his drink, 'he said he hoped it would be a case of third time lucky.'

'And it wasn't?' divined Henry Tyler without too much difficulty.

'Slipped through our fingers again on Saturday night.'

'Bad luck.'

'Oh, it can't be luck,' said Howkins at once. 'He must have a system. The only trouble is that we can't break it.'

'His luck may run out, though.' Henry Tyler felt he ought to make a pitch for Lady Luck, who had come to the aid of the Foreign Office more often than he liked to think about.

'I'd rather ours held,' said Howkins, demonstrating that policemen could play with words too. 'I shouldn't think we'll get many more chances with this fellow.'

'Slippery customer, eh?'

'Let me tell you this much, Tyler . . .'

Henry bent his head forward attentively although there

were no guests within earshot. The Mordaunt Club members themselves had an unbroken history of total discretion which was implicit and not enjoined upon them. It was in the tradition of the seventeenth-century country gentleman after whom the club was named: and was one of the many points which figured in the thinking – if not in the Minutes – of the Committee during its deliberations on the ticklish question of the admission of women to the club.

The Commander said, 'It's not every day we get a chance of picking up the real brains behind a drug racket right here in the middle of London, I can tell you.'

'If criminals have got brains, then they use them,' agreed Henry Tyler.

'Let alone three chances,' said the Commander, lapsing back into melancholy.

It wasn't a question of brains that was making the question of the admission of women to the Mordaunt Club so tricky. Diehards were insisting that the question was academic (since women *per se* were seldom of a sufficiently Mordaunt cast of mind to qualify for membership) and the views of Sir John Mordaunt himself on the subject unknown (but not too difficult to conjecture).

'Ah,' said Henry Tyler, himself cast in the mould of Dreier's celebrated dictum of a diplomat being a man who thought twice before saying nothing. 'Shall you get a fourth chance, do you think?'

Howkins still looked depressed. 'Well, so far we've always known where to find him the weekend after a shipment comes in, which is something that doesn't happen in every case.'

'And do you always know when that is going to be?' enquired Tyler pertinently.

'Oh, yes, that's no trouble. Thanks to your people, actually. The local Brit-bod in Lasserta usually tips us off in good time.'

Something in Henry's expression caused the Commander to rephrase this. 'Sorry,' he grinned. 'That's short-speak for Her Britannic Majesty's Ambassador to the Sheikhdom of Lasserta.'

'Anthony Heber Hibbs?'

'That's him. He's got a pretty good intelligence system going out there where they make the stuff so that's no problem.'

'So what is?' Identifying the problem was always important. Even if nothing could be done about it. That was part of the working credo in Henry's department.

'Evidence, lack of and need for,' said Howkins cogently. 'It's got to be stone-cold, straight-up and irrefutable evidence before we blow our cover or we've lost everything and then we'll never catch him.'

'You want him red-handed,' said Henry, falling back on an earlier phrasing. It was one which Sir John Mordaunt would have understood.

'We do.' The Commander started on his whitebait. 'And we want him rather badly.'

'I can see you don't want just small fry either,' agreed Henry Tyler, who had opted for *hors-d'oeuvres* rather than whitebait. 'Small fry aren't worth losing your set-up for.'

'Let's face it,' said Howkins. 'Our cover can't be all that good or someone wouldn't be giving him the nod every time we close in but for what it's worth we'd like to try to keep our cover and nobble whoever's doing the Sister Ann act.'

'What Sherlock Holmes would have called a three-pipe problem . . .'

'More like half a dozen hookahs,' said Howkins, getting pessimistic again. 'I've been racking my brains all weekend.'

'He – your chappie – can't be too worried about walking into a trap, then, can he?'

The Foreign Office man didn't get a direct answer. 'Have

you ever heard, Tyler, of a famous restaurant in Manlow Street?'

' "Mother Carey's Chickens"? Oh, yes . . .'

'Well, we established first of all that our man has regular meetings at "Les Poulets de la Mère Carey" there the week after a shipment of heroin comes in from the Sheikhdom.'

'Then he is doing well, your drugs baron,' said Henry. 'It must be one of the most expensive eating places in Town.'

'That's what our auditors say, too,' said Howkins. 'They've even suggested we weren't nobbling our suspect too soon because we liked eating there too.'

'Men without souls, auditors,' observed Henry.

'If I could only work out how he knows when to walk out of Mère Carey's empty-handed and when not to, then I'd be a happy man.'

'Because you could then catch him dealing,' agreed Henry.

'Which he would only do if he didn't know we were there.' The Commander sounded injured. 'It's not only that. It's the cocking a snook aspect that gets me, too.'

'He's doing a Queen Anne's Fan on you,' said Henry Tyler calmly.

The Commander looked mystified. 'I know she's dead, Tyler, but . . .'

'Putting your thumb to your nose with your fingers spread out is pure Queen Anne.'

'Queen Anne?'

'None other. Her reign was a time of much politicking and snoot-cocking, as our revered namesake Mordaunt found out.'

'Really? Well, as far as I'm concerned the farther police are from politics the better.'

'There weren't any police then.'

64

'No heroin either, though,' said the Commander, still licking his wounds.

The arrival of an ashet of rare beef temporarily put paid to conversation.

'This man of yours . . .' resumed Henry presently.

'Sharp as a barrel-load of monkeys and the mentality of a buccaneer . . .'

Yes, it would be the latter that rankled, thought Tyler to himself.

'Carrying on his business in one of the best restaurants in London before our very eyes.'

'Which means he has a high-class clientele.'

'That's part of the problem,' said the Commander. 'Before we know where we are, Tyler, we'll be getting questions asked in the House. And you don't need me to tell you where that can lead to.'

'No.' Howkins was talking to a man to whom the phrase struck home hard. Tyler glanced up at a portrait of Sir John hanging on the wall. Politics had been simpler in Mordaunt's day. In the words of his biographer, 'As a country squire, John must automatically have supported the one Established Church, agricultural rather than commercial interests, and peace rather than war.' Parliamentary life wasn't as uncomplicated as that any more.

'We just can't fathom who tips Chummie the wink,' said Howkins, pushing his plate away.

'The head waiter?' suggested Henry, sometimes – but not always – a believer in going straight to the top.

'Believe you me, Caesar's wife is nothing in comparison,' responded Howkins. 'Hippolyte Chatout's been with Mother Carey's man and boy, and as far as we can make out he's as honest as they come. Well,' the Commander amended this thoughtfully, 'as far as head waiters come.'

'One of the other waiters, then . . .'

Howkins sighed. 'We've had a couple of those fancy microphones under the tablecloth of our laddie's reserved table and never once picked up anything in the way of a warning.'

'A message in the menu?'

'Not that our cipher people can find,' said the policeman wearily.

'A message in a bottle, then?' suggested Tyler. 'By the way, will you have a spot more yourself?'

The Commander shook his head. 'Thank you, no. The sommelier's French, too, and as clean as a whistle.'

Henry Tyler, though a Foreign Office man through and through, let that pass. 'He could have brought wine *a* when wine *b* had been ordered,' he said.

'We know it isn't him,' said Howkins, 'because our chappie got away twice while the sommelier was off sick so he's in the clear anyway.'

'The hat-check girl?'

'Our villain's always already on his way before he gets near Monique.'

'Madame herself?'

Commander Howkins looked properly shocked. 'Madame Therese de l'Aubigny-Febeaux feels very strongly the pleasures of the table to be superior to those of any drugs and in any case she insists that she has first of all her reputation to think of.'

'Quite so,' murmured Henry.

'She has been most accommodating,' said Howkins warmly, 'and very co-operative with the Force . . .'

'I'm glad to hear it,' said Henry, whose whole training was to prefer '*entente*' to '*détente*'.

'Most accommodating – except, naturally, in the matter of expenses.'

'Naturally,' agreed Henry Tyler, who in his day, had

served time on the Paris desk in the Foreign Office. 'Well, Howkins, then in my view that only leaves us, too, going the way of all flesh . . .'

'What was that, Tyler?'

'The way of all flesh,' quoted Henry in a manner very similar to Sir John Mordaunt, 'is to the kitchen.'

'Pudding, gentlemen?' The waiter at the Mordaunt had appeared at their elbows. The terms 'sweet' and 'dessert' were not used at the club. 'There's plum duff, raisin sponge and a very good blackberry and apple tart . . .'

As soon as important decisions in this matter had been taken, the Commander returned to worry at his own private bone. 'We've been over the kitchen staff, of course, but we just can't see how they could get a message to Chummie anyway. They never go into the restaurant.'

'But they know when you're there?'

The Commander nodded as he leaned a little to one side to allow a plate of raisin sponge to be placed before him. 'Bound to. It's the only place from which we can watch him without him seeing us. We have a couple of our people dining at the next table to him, too, but the kitchen's a line of escape we just have to keep covered.'

Henry Tyler's choice of pudding was an old-fashioned plum duff. 'Tell me about the food at Mother Carey's . . .'

'Very good, unless you go in for the fancy stuff. You know what I mean – half an ounce of fish in a pretty sauce, five shavings of carrot, three peas and a tomato all looking more like a painting than a proper meal.'

'Cuisine nouvelle.' His dining companion, no light-weight, nodded sadly.

'And what you might call "afters" is a slurp of syrup with three strawberries on a plate the size of your hand.' The Commander was tucking into his raisin sponge with purpose.

'So your man has a watcher in the kitchen, then?'

'Seems like it,' said the Commander, 'but we can't arrest the lot and anyway we need to know how the message is got across to catch our quarry. It's him we want, don't forget, and before he sees the writing on the wall.'

'And who's doing the cooking out there at the back?'

'Four chefs, three assistants, a couple of vegetable cooks and a slip of a girl who does the sweet course and nothing else.'

Henry considered his plum duff thoughtfully. Then he lifted his face, a seraphic smile on his countenance. 'The writing isn't on the wall, old man.'

'No?'

'It's on the *Pave de Pastille* or something very like it.'

'What?'

'I'm prepared to wager ten ecus to a brass farthing,' said Henry grandly, 'that your drug dealer got his warning in cream.'

'Cream?'

'Written with a little stick across the blackcurrant coulis or whatever. It's not difficult . . .'

'But . . .' Howkins' spoon was suspended over the last of his raisin sponge.

'It would be something very simple, of course. Probably a word like "scram" or "flee" or even,' he added unkindly, 'seeing that it's a French restaurant, "cochons" . . .'

'And no one except the waiter would see it,' said the Commander, slapping his thigh. 'I've got you. Nouvelle, indeed! I'll make mincemeat of him next time. That's not French, is it, Tyler?'

Cause and Effects

'OF COURSE you must come with us, Henry, dear. I insist. Besides, Margot will be so pleased.'

'I really don't see why any hostess should be pleased to see a total stranger arrive at her dinner party.' Henry Tyler had had an unexpected few days' leave and had descended on his married sister and her husband in the small market town of Berebury in Calleshire without a great deal of warning.

'You're not a total stranger . . .'

'To my certain knowledge, Wendy, I have never set eyes on anyone called Margot Iverson in my life before.'

'I know that,' said Wendy Witherington placidly, 'but you're my brother and that's the same as my knowing her or her knowing me.' Logic had never been Wendy's strong suit.

'I still don't see why she should be pleased to see me on Saturday evening,' said Henry mildly.

'Because you're a man, that's why.'

'And may I ask why she will be so delighted to see me because I happen to be a male member of the human race . . . ?' There was nothing in his face to show how much he enjoyed teasing his only sister. 'Or is it only that I don't understand why as a consequence of being a mere male?'

Henry worked at the Foreign Office in London where ambiguity had been raised to an art form. Wendy's mind was a much more literal one.

'Because you're an extra man, dear,' she said.

'Ah.'

'And because of Arthur's Cousin Amy,' went on his sister. 'She always upsets the table.'

'Dipsomania?' enquired Henry Tyler with interest. 'Or is she just a clairvoyant?'

'Don't be unkind,' said Wendy severely. 'Cousin Amy can't help being there. She hasn't anywhere else to go but The Hollies.'

'She doesn't always have to upset the table, though, when she is there, does she?' remarked Henry Tyler in a tone that at least one ambassador had been known to call 'eminently reasonable'.

'Arthur's Cousin Amy,' responded his sister firmly, 'works as a secretary at a girls' boarding school. She's as poor as a church mouse, that's why she has to come to Arthur and Margot's in the holidays.'

'And what happens,' asked Henry mischievously, 'when Cousin Amy isn't there and your friends have an extra man?'

'Oh, that's no problem,' said Wendy at once. 'Margot just asks Miss Chalder to stay on. She's Arthur's dispenser and receptionist. Young but quite presentable.'

'So Arthur's a doctor . . .' divined Henry without too much difficulty.

'Oh, didn't I say? He's our general practitioner.' Wendy giggled. 'Actually when she's not there Margot calls Miss Chalder their deceptionist.'

'Always saying the doctor's out when he's in?' Deception was another of the subjects that they knew rather a lot about at the Foreign Office. 'That sort of thing?'

'And saying,' said Wendy, 'that he's been held up at a confinement when he's forgotten all about somebody.'

'Is he a good doctor?' asked Henry. It wasn't entirely an

idle question since Wendy and Tom Witherington had two young children upon whom their bachelor uncle doted.

'How does one ever know that, Henry?' Wendy had more intelligence than her pleasant calm looks might have led the casual observer to suspect. She wrinkled her brow. 'There was some trouble at the end of last year about a little gypsy child who died from a burst appendix. Arthur said he'd never had their second message and the fuss all died down but he's always come when we've sent for him.'

'Quite so,' said Henry Tyler. 'I shall look forward to Saturday evening, then.'

'And I shall telephone Margot,' said his sister.

Later that evening Henry, who was a firm believer that time spent in reconnaissance was seldom wasted, raised the matter of the dinner party with his brother-in-law.
'Don't worry, old chap.' Tom Witherington was reassuring. 'They do you very well at The Hollies. Very well indeed.'

'So Dr Iverson is a successful doctor,' murmured Henry Tyler (which he knew was not the same as being a good one).

Tom Witherington frowned. 'Couldn't say, but he is sound on food and drink.'

'How is it that their entertaining is so – er – reliable, then?'

'Oh, you mean how is it that they can afford the pukka style if he isn't successful?' His brother-in-law's brow cleared. 'That's easily explained. W. H. M.'

Henry Tyler thought for a moment. 'That's an acronym I haven't come across.'

Tom Witherington grinned. 'I don't suppose it matters in the Foreign Office as much as it does in some other spheres. W. H. M. stands for "Wife Has Means" ... Margot has the money and Arthur has the ideas for using it. You'll see on Saturday.'

'I can hardly wait,' said Henry Tyler politely.

As dinner parties went, noted Henry on the night, it was neither large nor particularly intimate. Ten people sat down in the dining-room at The Hollies after partaking of a well-chosen sherry – a good Macharnudo, Henry thought – in the drawing-room.

Margot Iverson had welcomed him most hospitably. 'How nice to have someone here from the Foreign Office. You can tell us what they think of Il Duce.' She was a plain woman with the apparent placidity of the overweight but she didn't look as if she missed much. Like those of all good hostesses, her eyes were everywhere.

'I'm afraid,' said Henry Tyler with every appearance of regret, 'that's not my department.'

Dr Iverson was equally welcoming. 'What a pity it's dark. Otherwise you could have seen the garden, although there's not much to look at at this time of the year.'

'Arthur's garden is a delight,' said Wendy at his elbow. 'In the summer his vegetable garden is as neat and attractive as the one at Villandry.'

'It's mostly my gardener I have to thank for that,' said the doctor modestly, 'but, yes, I do take an interest. Now, let me introduce you to Major Anderson. He's the Chairman of our local Bench. . .'

The announcement about dinner being served, Henry observed with approval, had come at just the right length of time after the sherry had been drunk. It followed a brief absence from the room of the doctor.

'Just checking on the claret,' he boomed as he came back. 'Edith's very good but there are some things that need watching.'

'My cousin is something of a wine connoisseur, Mr Tyler,' said Miss Amy Hall as he escorted her in to dinner.

The doctor's cousin was a thin, anxious woman with her hair drawn down in two neat earphones. 'Now, tell me what you think of Haile Selassie . . .'

The first course had been awaiting them on the dining-room table. Potted shrimps in attractive little ramekins, and prettily adorned with watercress, stood on plates at each place. It was clear that the Major's wife was the chief lady guest as she was seated on Dr Iverson's right, the Major sitting on Margot Iverson's right.

A Mr and Mrs Locombe-Stableford made up the party. Henry had already discovered that he was a solicitor and his wife a power in the Red Cross. Henry found himself next to the Major's wife.

'I hope you enjoy your visit to Calleshire,' she said. 'A very fine county.'

'Indeed.' Henry passed her some thin, crustless brown bread and butter and listened to a long story about fox-hunting. Across the table he could hear Mrs Locombe-Stableford talking to the doctor about someone's gall-stones ('Seven as big as marbles, the surgeon said').

Edith, the parlour-maid, cleared away the first course.

'Jolly good tiger-frighteners, what?' said the Major to Margot Iverson.

'He usually calls them "horses' doovers",' sighed the Major's wife to Henry, 'which is worse.'

'Strange how we have taken to some French words and not others, isn't it?' remarked Henry diplomatically as the parlour-maid came into the room with a pile of dinner-plates and the vegetable dishes.

'I hope you'll take to a good French claret,' chimed in Arthur Iverson jovially. 'One of the St Émilion hill wines. Château Balestard la Tonnelle and just about ready for drinking . . . Ah, thank you, Edith. Put it down here. Carefully, now . . .'

Obediently the parlour-maid lowered a serving dish bearing a large fillet of beef on the table in front of the doctor. He put his hands out to take up the carving knife and fork and Amy Hall murmured something to her neighbour about Arthur always having wanted to be a surgeon really.

'My dear,' he said to his wife, 'aren't you going to tell our guests about our new addition to the dining-room?'

All eyes turned towards Margot Iverson at the other end of the dining table. She almost pouted. 'I wasn't going to tell them, Arthur. I was going to show them later.'

'Very well, my dear.' The doctor turned his attention back to the carving. He was indeed good at it. After having carefully removed the browned edge of the fillet he sliced the meat quickly and evenly. Edith took the plates to Margot Iverson's end of the table where the vegetables were served and then handed them in turn to the guests.

Henry passed the horseradish sauce and then the gravy to the Major's wife. 'And salt?' he enquired. The career of one of his Foreign Office contemporaries had been said to have foundered after he had said 'Pepper and salt' to the wife of a diplomat with uncertainly coloured hair and a poor command of the English language.

'Now you really must tell us what you think of the Abyssinian question, Mr Tyler,' Brenda Anderson said as soon as Edith had withdrawn.

'Dear lady, I am but an errand boy in the Foreign Service . . .' At the other end of the table he could hear Margot Iverson exchanging stately platitudes with Mr Locombe-Stableford. Henry Tyler would not have described her as a happy woman but afterwards he could not say that she had seemed at all unwell. She certainly complained of nothing in his hearing.

Her moment came at the end of the first course when, without any apparent signal, the parlour-maid came back into the room.

'There,' challenged Arthur. 'How did Margot summon up reinforcements? Tell me that if you can.'

'Perhaps,' suggested Tom Witherington slyly, 'Edith was listening at the door . . .'

'Did you hear that, Edith?' said Arthur Iverson. 'Well, were you?'

'No, doctor.'

'Bush telegraph?' The Major had served in Africa.

'Oh, do tell us,' pleaded Wendy Witherington. 'We'll never guess.'

'A bell-push under the carpet by my foot,' said Margot Iverson calmly. 'Arthur got an electrician to do it during the week.'

'Clever stuff,' exclaimed Tom as Edith bought in the puddings.

She placed a hot Normandy pudding for the doctor to serve and a *crème brûlée* for her mistress to offer to those who preferred it.

'A great nation, the French,' said Mrs Locombe-Stableford, eyeing the puddings.

'In some ways, yes,' said Henry, a Foreign Office man to his fingertips even on Saturday evenings. 'But not all.'

'You mustn't forget Cook's special wine sauce with the Normandy pudding,' said Margot Iverson. 'She's very proud of it.'

'Or the Barsac,' said Dr Iverson. 'I think the ladies will like it . . .'

It was late by the time the meal was done and later still when the company rose from the coffee cups in the drawing-room.

It was early, though, the next morning when Wendy Witherington came back from the telephone. 'That was Brenda Anderson,' she said, looking shocked. 'You won't believe this but Margot Iverson died in the night . . .'

'No! Surely not . . .' exclaimed Tom.

'What on earth from?' asked Henry.

'Brenda doesn't know,' said Wendy, 'but apparently poor Margot started being sick about one o'clock in the morning and then had a most frightful pain in her tummy.'

'At least Arthur would have been there,' said her husband. 'Nothing like having a doctor in the house.'

'He got very worried and immediately sent for one of the consultants from the hospital.'

'I should think so . . .' murmured Henry.

'And the consultant wanted to know what she'd had to eat, of course . . .'

'Of course.' Tom Witherington looked very solemn.

'And whether anyone else had been taken ill.'

'Naturally,' said Henry.

'They were just going to check that we were all right when Margot suddenly got quite excitable and delirious – so unlike her.'

Henry nodded. Margot Iverson had struck him as a very controlled woman.

'And then' – Wendy's voice began to quaver – 'her breathing got very slow. Brenda says she was in a coma by the time they got her into the hospital. And then she just died . . . Oh, isn't it too awful?'

Both men nodded.

Wendy sniffed. 'I think I'll just ring Phyllis Locombe-Stableford . . .'

'No,' said Tom Witherington quietly. 'I don't think I would if I were you, Wendy.'

'Why ever not?' Wendy stared at her husband. 'She was there too last night.'

'That's why,' said Tom. 'And she may not want to talk about it. Or have been asked not to by her husband . . .' He put his arm round his wife. 'I think you're forgetting something about old Locombe-Stableford.'

She was close to tears now. 'What's that?'

'That he isn't only a solicitor.' Tom went on steadily: 'He's the Coroner as well.'

Beyond speech now, she nodded her comprehension. 'Brenda said they were doing a post-mortem examination this morning. Oh, poor, poor Margot . . .'

Henry Tyler said: 'I have to be back in Whitehall tomorrow, Wen. I must be with my Minister at ten but I'll come back for the funeral . . . or if anyone else wants to talk to me . . .'

In the event the persons who wanted to talk to Henry Tyler went to the Foreign Office to see him – where they found his rank to be rather higher than that of errand-boy. In fact he had his own office and a considerably larger area of carpet than anyone in Berebury suspected.

The two policemen who were shown into his room did not appear to be daunted by this. 'Detective Inspector Milsom,' said the senior of the pair, 'and my assistant, Detective Constable Bewman. We are making enquiries into the sudden death of Mrs Margot Iverson.'

Henry Tyler bowed his head. 'Anything I can tell you, Inspector, I will, but my acquaintanceship with Mrs Iverson in the event was brief.'

'It is the event,' said Milsom drily, 'which interests us. You were, I understand, one of the guests on the fatal night . . .'

'Indeed,' said Henry, noting with the appreciation of an expert the Inspector's choice of words.

'And partook of the complete meal?'

'Oh, yes, Inspector. And very good it was, too.'

'Save for Mrs Iverson, sir. It didn't do her any good at all. Quite the reverse, you might say.'

'Are you telling me,' said Henry cautiously, 'that Mrs Iverson – er – consumed . . . '

'Ingested was the word the Home Office pathologist used, sir.'

'Ingested that from which she died at that meal?'

'It would seem so, sir. And we want you to tell us everything you remember about it.'

Henry cast his mind back over the evening. 'I think we all ate the same . . .'

'That is one of the things that is making our enquiries difficult.' Detective Inspector Milsom had his notebook at the ready.

'And from the same dishes . . . no, I forgot. The first course was on the table when we went into the diningroom. Potted shrimps.' He looked sharply at the policeman. 'Shell-fish can be dangerous in their own right.'

'The potted shrimps were put on the table by the parlourmaid immediately before the guests entered the diningroom,' said Milsom.

Henry hesitated but not for long. 'Our host did slip out to attend to the claret . . .'

'That was before the shrimp dish reached the diningroom,' said Milsom, revealing that he already knew a great deal about the evening. 'It was – er – safely in the kitchen at that stage.'

'And,' said Henry as lightly as he felt the conversation warranted, 'I suppose you are sure that Edith wasn't harbouring a grudge against her mistress.'

'As sure as we can be,' said Milsom.

Detective Constable Bewman stirred. 'Besides, if you remember, sir, the potted shrimps had a solidified butter glaze on top.'

'So it had,' said Henry appreciatively. The constabulary had certainly done its homework. 'And Mrs Iverson would certainly have noticed if that had been disturbed.'

'I think we can go a little further than that, sir.' Milsom

gave a faint smile. 'Human nature being what it is my guess is that any maid worth her salt would have put a slightly imperfect dish in front of anyone but her master or mistress for the cook's sake.'

'Quite so,' said Henry gravely. He had forgotten the old joke about a policeman being the best kitchen range-finder in the world. 'Well, apart from the potted shrimps I think I can assure you, Inspector, that one way and another all the other dishes were shared.'

'This is what all the other guests say, sir, and that is what is puzzling us.'

'What about after we all left?' said Henry.

'The experts assure us that symptoms occur between one and four hours after this particular substance has been ingested.' The Detective Inspector went on in tones totally devoid of emphasis: 'Unfortunately Dr Iverson went out after the dinner-party to pay a late visit to a man with pneumonia about whom he was worried and so cannot tell us anything about the time immediately after the guests had left. By the time he got home his wife was already beginning to be unwell.'

'I see.' Henry frowned. 'Well, after the potted shrimps we had the beef – and very good it was, too.'

'I understand that Cook has an excellent relationship with the butcher. She got him to send round the largest and best fillet he had,' said Milsom.

'The vegetables, as I recollect, Inspector, were Brussels sprouts and glazed carrots.' The man on the Belgium desk at the Foreign Office was being driven to despair by what was coming out of Brussels at the moment but Henry saw no reason to say so.

'We think we can give the vegetables a clean bill of health, sir.'

'Finished up in the kichen, were they?' divined Henry.

'I say, Inspector, what about the horseradish sauce? It brought a tear to my eye.'

'Home-made, Mr Tyler, by Cook, according to Mrs Beeton's recipe, with cream, white wine vinegar, a little caster sugar and some mustard – and horseradish, of course.'

'I have heard,' said Henry slowly, 'that on occasion – by accident, usually – aconite has been known to have been mistaken for horseradish.'

'Picked by Cook herself in the kitchen garden,' said Inspector Milsom with evident approval. 'She says that when she asks the gardener for produce she feels she doesn't always get the best.'

'Human nature doesn't change, does it?' said Henry absently. They knew quite as much about human nature at the Foreign Office as they did down at any police station. 'Besides, coming back to your problem, Inspector, nearly everybody had some of the horseradish sauce.'

'Exactly, sir. Our problem is that while Mrs Iverson appears to have ingested that from which she died at the dinner party there is no dish which some or all the guests did not share.'

'Difficult,' agreed Henry, 'and made more so, I imagine, by the fact that both the Coroner and the Chairman of the Magistrates' Bench were there.'

Detective Inspector Milsom said with deep feeling that this had not helped in the investigation so far. 'They both insist that there was no way in which their hostess could have been poisoned before their very eyes – and both the parlour-maid and the cook swear that she didn't take anything afterwards. What with the doctor going straight out and the deceased going down to the kitchen to thank both staff for a very good meal there wasn't time – even if she took it herself, which is unlikely from all I hear.'

'That means Edith and Cook liked her,' said Henry at once. 'And I understand there were no money troubles . . .'

'None,' said the Inspector stoutly. 'She was very well off, was Mrs Iverson.'

'And yet . . .' began Henry.

'Yes?' The policeman leaned forward.

'It does seem almost staged, doesn't it?'

'Just what the Chief Constable said . . .' The Detective Inspector lowered his head. 'I'm sorry, sir, I shouldn't have said that.'

Henry Tyler waved a hand airily. 'My dear fellow, we spend our time here working on things that shouldn't have been said, but unless they are,' he added thoughtfully, 'nobody gets anywhere. That case of pneumonia?'

'Genuine,' said the Inspector. 'The doctor had visited the man earlier in the day and said he would be back later that night when he thought the pneumonia would have reached its crisis.'

'Mrs Iverson hadn't been beastly to Miss Amy Hall, I take it?'

'Kindness itself, I understand, sir.' He coughed. 'That doesn't mean that Miss Hall enjoys being a poor relation. Very few people do, sir. However, both staff agree Miss Hall fitted in as well as anyone could in the circumstances. Cook is a most observant woman and parlour-maids have to be of a noticing cast of mind otherwise they wouldn't be any good for the job, would they, sir?'

Henry confessed it was something that hadn't crossed his mind before.

'Like detective constables,' said the Inspector generously. 'Constable Bewman here pointed out that each guest had their plate handed to them by Edith but I can't see how that gave a murderer any scope.'

Henry frowned. 'She would have done it in a preordained

way, of course,' he mused. 'The lady on the host's right first, and then the one on his left. My sister was served after them, I think, and then Miss Amy and Mrs Iverson.'

'That would have meant,' said the Inspector alertly, 'that anyone who knew where you were all sitting would have been able to work out who would get which plate in the pile.'

'Oh, yes, Inspector.' Henry Tyler smiled faintly. 'It's an interesting little puzzle when you think about it like that. The quickness of the hand deceiving the eye and all that. Except that we don't know whose hand.'

'Yet . . .' responded Milsom.

Detective Constable Bewman scratched his head. 'But even if you knew beforehand who was going to get – say – the fifth plate how could you put poison on it and not on the other plates?'

'Difficult,' agreed Henry Tyler, 'isn't it?'

'But not impossible,' growled Milsom. 'According to the pathologist, the timing is wrong for her being poisoned except at the meal. He's prepared to swear to that.'

Henry Tyler screwed up his eyes in an effort of recollection. 'There were some glazed onions and Duchesse potatoes round the fillet . . . our host put those on the individual plates before he handed them to Edith.'

'We thought of that, sir,' said the Inspector, a touch of melancholy in his voice. 'Both were brought in from the garden – home grown – and never left the kitchen until Cook gave them to Edith for the table. Apparently the doctor's very particular about his potatoes. Never lets seed be used that's more than two years out of Scotland.'

'Quite right,' said Henry stoutly. 'I think the same should go for the Scots race, too.'

'Not everyone had the same pudding,' said the Inspector with a certain tenacity. 'Some had one and some had the other.'

'And some, Inspector, I fear, had both.'

'And those that had the Normandy pudding,' said Detective Constable Bewman, 'had the wine sauce that went with it.'

'It was a splendid sauce,' said Henry appreciatively.

'Consisting, I understand,' said Milsom heavily, 'of a small glass of brandy, ditto of Madeira, a gill of water, an ounce of unsalted butter and a little caster sugar.'

'You should try it sometime, Inspector,' said Henry.

'It was handed round,' said Milsom, ignoring this frivolity, 'by Edith in a sauce boat on a tray.'

'No room for monkey business there,' agreed Henry. 'Or with the fruit and nuts.'

'Two bowls of each were placed within easy reach of all the guests,' said Milsom. 'In theory I suppose the nearest piece of fruit could have been doctored but I don't see myself how the murderer could have been sure the victim would have picked it.'

'No.' Henry noted how the Detective Inspector's speech had now widened to include words like 'poison' and 'murderer'. 'I can't tell you if Mrs Iverson had any port.' He grinned. 'I did and it was splendid.'

'Vintage,' said Milsom. 'Nineteen twelve and nothing wrong with it at all.'

'Just as well to check, though,' agreed Henry gravely.

'The doctor had decanted it himself,' the policeman informed him, reddening slightly, 'before the guests arrived.'

'You can't be too careful with a really crusty port,' said Henry.

'Someone,' said Inspector Milsom meaningfully, 'seems to have been altogether too careful, to my way of thinking.'

Henry Tyler nodded. 'Careful and very clever, Inspector. It takes a great deal of prestidigitatory skill to poison someone before your very eyes, so to speak.'

'That's not a word that I know, sir, but I think I take your meaning.'

'We are talking of the art of the conjuror . . .'

'Ah,' said Milsom.

'Where did the patter come in, then?' enquired Detective Constable Bewman. 'You would have all been talking normally like, wouldn't you, sir?'

'Yes . . . that is, I suppose so.' Henry cast his mind back to the small talk of a small town. 'Conversation was very general. The nearest thing to a conjuring trick was the new bell-push that had been fitted under the carpet for Mrs Iverson.'

'That was the doctor's idea, sir. Cook tells me he'd seen it somewhere and wanted one for his wife. The parlour-maid likes it because it saves her . . .'

'Just a minute,' said Henry, a thought beginning to burgeon in his mind. 'You, Constable, said something about a conjuror's patter.'

'You don't get that many silent ones, sir,' responded Bewman stolidly. 'Not on stage, anyway.'

'It did occur to me that the doctor did choose an odd moment to draw attention to the bell's being there. It would have been much more subtle just to have allowed his wife to demonstrate it when the time came and then to turn it into a talking point.'

'Out of character you might say?' suggested the Inspector. 'And what, might I ask, sir, was he doing at the time he was talking about the bell?'

'Oh, he wasn't doing the talking at that point, Inspector. It was Mrs Iverson who was telling us about it after he mentioned it.'

'So,' reasoned the Inspector, 'all the guests were looking at her?'

'I suppose we were.'

'So,' said Milsom patiently, 'what was the doctor doing while she was talking?'

Henry Tyler cast his mind back to the fatal evening. 'He was carving the fillet of beef. He'd just begun. He took off the first slice – you know, the rather well-done, brown bit at the end – and laid it on one side of the serving dish and then he cut the next slice off for the first lady and so on.'

'We can't work out how he could have killed his wife while he was sitting at the opposite end of the table,' said Constable Bewman naïvely.

'You have rather got it in for the doctor, haven't you?' said Henry easily.

'It's common knowledge that most male murderers are widowers,' growled Milsom. 'What we don't like, Mr Tyler, is that Mrs Iverson was poisoned in full view of the Coroner and the Chairman of the Bench.'

' "Aye, there's the rub," as William Shakespeare so wisely said,' murmured Henry.

'And Miss Chalder is a very good-looking girl.'

'Ah, so that's the way the wind blows, is it?' said Henry, his mind beginning to stray. 'Mind you,' he added fairly, 'doctors are able to get their hands on poison more easily than most of us.'

'Oh, didn't I say, Mr Tyler? It wasn't a medical poison that was used to kill Mrs Iverson.'

'No?' If Henry thought that there was a contradiction in terms about the words 'medical poison' he did not let it show in his face.

'More of a horticultural poison,' said the Inspector, 'although not intended as such.' He consulted his notebook. 'The substance was called ethylene chlorohydrin, if that means anything to you, sir.'

'I'm afraid not,' said Henry regretfully.

'Used to speed the germination of seeds and potatoes,'

said the Inspector, 'and as a cleaning solvent.'

'And it's odourless,' chimed in Constable Bewman helpfully.

'So there was no need to have anything highly scented or smelling strongly on the table,' said Henry at once.

'I hope you never take it into your head to commit a murder, sir,' said the Inspector. 'You do seem to have an eye for essentials.'

'And how much of this – er – horticultural poison does it take to kill a human being?' asked Henry, ignoring this last.

'Not a lot,' said the Inspector quietly. 'Something under a fifth of a teaspoonful – say four or five drops – added to which it is highly soluble.'

'It seems to me,' said Henry Tyler, in the last analysis a Ministry man, 'that this stuff, whatever it is, is something that ought to be put a stop to.'

'Very possibly, sir,' said the Inspector smoothly. 'And after the fruit and nuts?'

'We all moved back into the drawing-room for coffee,' said Henry, 'and I performed my party trick with the cream and the back of the spoon.' He looked up. 'It's not a conjuring trick, Inspector.'

'I'm glad to hear it, sir.'

'It's a question of how to get the cream to float on top of the coffee.'

'Very difficult, I'm sure, sir.'

'Not when you know how.'

'I think that is going to be the case with the ethylene chlorohydrin, sir.'

'Er – quite, Inspector. Well, with the coffee it's all a matter of putting the sugar in first and stirring well. That increases the surface tension on the top of the coffee – or is it the specific gravity? – so that when you dribble the cream slowly over the back of the spoon it stays on the top.'

'And Bob's your uncle, so to speak?' said the Inspector, paying unconscious tribute to an old nepotism.

'It worked,' said Henry. 'Whether it distracted everyone else long enough to slip five drops of something into Mrs Iverson's coffee, I wouldn't know, Inspector.'

'But we would, Mr Tyler. You see, Mrs Iverson never drank coffee. And we have it on the authority of those sitting near her that she did not drink it that evening.' He coughed. 'If I may say so, your sister was particularly emphatic on the point.'

'Good old Wendy,' said Henry. He frowned. 'I say, Inspector, that does rather leave every avenue explored, doesn't it?'

Detective Inspector Milsom assented to this sentiment with a quiet nod. 'Every avenue that we can think of.'

'What we want, Inspector,' he said bracingly, 'is a new avenue or a fresh look at an old one.'

'Either would do very nicely, sir.' With an ironic smile Milsom said: 'Which do you recommend?'

'Oh, a new look at an old problem,' said Henry Tyler at once. 'We don't have new problems in the Foreign Office.'

'The only matter which you have brought to our attention, sir, which seems to have escaped everyone else's notice was the – er – untimely mention of the footbell.'

'Which doesn't get us very much furth— Wait a minute, Inspector, wait a minute.'

'Yes, sir?'

'Suppose it does?' Henry ran his hands through his hair in a gesture of excitement that his sister would have recognized well. 'Suppose it was meant to turn all eyes towards our hostess?'

'And take them off your host?' said Milsom astringently.

'Exactly!'

'Well?'

'Well, if it was intended as a distraction, then that must have been the moment when he poisoned his wife. That follows, doesn't it?'

'It's a thought worth considering, sir.'

'Watch out, Inspector, if you can talk like that in response to one of my brainwaves we'll have you working here.'

'No, thank you, sir. We've got enough troubles of our own in Calleshire.'

'I think you're going to have one less in a minute.' He brought his fist down on his desk with a bang. 'Inspector, until this moment I have always felt that the benefit of a classical education was over-rated.'

'Indeed, sir?'

'But not now! Parysatis, wife of Darius, killed Statira, the wife of Artaxerxes, in much the same way as Margot Iverson was murdered.'

Detective Inspector Milsom leaned forward, his notebook prominent. 'Tell me . . .'

'Now I know what else it was Dr Iverson did when he went through to see to the claret before dinner.' Henry rubbed his hands. 'First he probably smeared a little horseradish sauce or even some colourless Vaseline on the right-hand side of the carving knife. He then added a fatal dose of your ethylene stuff to it and put it back on the carving rest . . .'

'With the other blade facing upward.' Detective Constable Bewman could hardly contain his excitement. Then his face fell. 'But why didn't the first guest get the poisoned beef?'

Detective Inspector Milsom said quietly, 'Because the doctor laid the first slice of the fillet – the browned outside piece that you don't give to guests – to one side of the carving dish . . . Mr Tyler said so.'

'But put it on his wife's plate later without anyone noticing,' said Henry. 'Only the left-hand side of the carving knife touched everyone else's meat.' He sat back in his chair. 'Parysatis did it with a chicken and I should have thought of it before.'

The Hard Sell

'MORNING, HARRY.' Detective Inspector Sloan shifted his chair an inch or two to indicate to Inspector Harpe that there was room to sit beside him at the table in the police canteen.

'Morning.' The Inspector from Traffic set a mug of tea and a pile of ham sandwiches down on the table and pulled up a chair.

Sloan let him settle to food and drink before asking cautiously: 'How's life?'

'Busy,' he said, taking a bite.

This was not an unexpected reply since Inspector Harpe was head of 'F' Division's Traffic Department and thus never without work. In addition to this he maintained a ceaseless campaign against drinking and driving – and an even more bitter one against those lawyers and magistrates whose view of what constituted random breath-testing did not coincide with his own.

Detective Inspector Sloan let the tea and sandwiches exert their customary beneficial effect on Harpe's temper before venturing further comment.

'All well in your neck of the woods?' he enquired presently. 'Like the motorway?' After drinking drivers Inspector Harpe reserved his ferocity for fast ones and was in the habit of referring to Calleshire's short stretch of motorway as The Route of All Evil.

Happy Harry grunted. 'Had a fatal last night.'

Sloan nodded sympathetically. This, no doubt, accounted for some of his colleague's taciturnity. Road traffic accidents, however trivial, were never exactly fun and where there was a death involved they were even less nice and, no matter what anyone said, policemen never did get inured to them. He said, 'There's always too many RTAs . . .'

'This wasn't exactly a road traffic accident.' Harry frowned. 'At least not within the meaning of the Act.'

'How come that you got it, then?' asked Detective Inspector Sloan, professionally curious.

'The caller said there'd been a car accident and so naturally we attended.'

'And had there?'

'Oh, yes, there had been a car accident, all right,' responded Harpe simply, 'and it was certainly death by motor car. I'll grant you that.'

'I wonder how the statisticians will deal with it, then,' mused Sloan. He'd never felt the same way about statisticians since he'd heard about the one who had drowned in a river whose average depth was six inches . . .

'It's not the numbers game that I'm interested in,' snorted Harpe.

Sloan toyed with the idea of repeating the old joke about statisticians to Happy Harry but decided against it. Instead he asked: 'What happened, then?'

'Funniest thing,' said Harpe. 'It was at this meeting of the Calleshire Classic Car Club. They have their get-togethers at . . .'

'I know,' said Sloan. 'Down at the old railway goods yard.'

'More's the pity,' said Harpe: this was another beef of the Traffic Inspector's. 'Now if all the freight went by goods wagon on the railways we'd have half the traffic and a quarter of the problems we get on the roads.'

'And if all the population stuck to the Ten Commandments,' said the Head of 'F' Division's Criminal Investigation Department, 'then I'd be out of a job. What happened, Harry?'

'Well, you know the goods yard as well as I do. They've still got some old platforms down there even though they've taken up the tracks as well as the waste ground where the old railway sidings used to be . . .'

'Berebury North Station,' supplied Sloan. 'That was.'

'Closed by the good Dr Beeching, I suppose . . .'

'No,' said Sloan, who was Calleshire born and bred. 'Berebury North closed before the war when the fish trade fell away. The herring failed. What happened yesterday?'

'Well, they were using the old railway down platform to show off these classic cars. They don't make them like that any more, Sloan. Beautiful jobs, they are. You should have seen the old Aston Martin they had there. Now there's a car with everything . . .'

'What happened?'

But there was no rushing the Traffic man: he might have been making a statement to the court, his tale was so measured. 'They'd just got the cars all lined up in a row with their front wheels right up to the edge of the platform so that they could have their photographs taken for some magazine. Lovely to see proper bodywork and real chrome . . .'

'Best side to London if it was the down platform,' observed Sloan.

Irony was always wasted on Inspector Harpe who paused, searching for a good simile. 'Like so many race horses.'

'Were they showing their paces too?' enquired Sloan. 'And pawing the ground?'

'There's no need to be sarcastic, Sloan. They all go – it's

just that they don't go far or so fast these days.'

'No different really then from any other geriatrics, eh?' Sloan took a drink from his own cup. 'And do I take it, Harry, that one of them went far enough to kill someone?'

The Traffic Inspector nodded, his mouth full of sandwich. 'Sort of,' he mumbled.

'While it was on the down platform?'

The nod was even more vigorous this time.

'It went over the platform?' divined Sloan.

'That's right.' The sandwich had gone down red lane now. 'A pearl grey 1961 2.4 Jaguar came off over the edge and fell on to a chap who was thinking of buying it.' A rare flash of humour burgeoned over Happy Harry's melancholy features. 'He bought it all right.'

'Who was at the wheel?'

'Didn't I say, Sloan? That was the interesting thing. No one.'

'No one?'

'As many witnesses as any court could want are ready and willing to swear to there having been no one – but no one – in the car when it moved forward. First thing they looked at – after sending for us and the ambulance, of course.'

'What about the engine?'

'Ticking over in drive. You see, the owner – a man by the name of Daniel White – was trying to persuade the deceased to take the Jaguar in settlement of some betting debt and was making him listen to how sweet the engine sounded when it took this great leap forward like the Chinese under Mao Tse Tung.'

'Did the throttle-return spring snap?' suggested Sloan, whose interest in foreign affairs wasn't as far-reaching as it should have been. His grandfather had always worried about the Yellow Peril: he was more interested in a newly killed man. 'Metal fatigue must be a problem in those old things.'

'First thing we checked after we'd got the boy out from under,' grunted Harpe. 'Right as ninepence – the throttle-return spring, I mean. Ned Tolland was dead.'

'I see.'

'Mind you, he must have been just in front of the Jag at the time it hit him and a good three feet below it . . .'

'Why?'

'White said he wanted Tolland to stand there to hear the engine running – if he could.'

'Why shouldn't he have heard it?' asked Sloan. 'Was he deaf or something?'

Inspector Harpe looked disappointed. 'Don't you remember that old ad about the Rolls-Royce clock being the only thing you could hear when the engine was running or something?'

'Harry, I'm not a motor man and I'm not an advertising man, just a plain old-fashioned policeman, detective branch. What about the brakes?'

'I think,' said Inspector Harpe judiciously, 'you could say that the brakes were half on.'

'Or half off,' observed Detective Inspector Sloan detachedly.

'Not that that should have made all that difference,' said Harpe. 'According to an independent witness – the owner of the next car along – an old Armstrong Siddeley – paint-work still black as night – they built cars to last in those days, Sloan . . .'

'The witness . . .' Sloan reminded him. He himself was never prepared to describe any witness, sight unseen, as independent but then, he would have been the first to admit, he was in the detective branch.

'The witness said that the engine of the Jaguar had been

running for quite a little while before the car moved forward apparently all on its own.'

'Odd,' agreed Sloan thoughtfully.

'Apparently Ned Tolland. . .'

'The victim,' said Sloan. There was, after all, no doubt about that.

'Him,' said Harpe ungrammatically. 'Apparently he hadn't been all that keen on taking the car in the first place. He'd already got an old Lanchester, you see, and anyway the car was worth more than what White owed him.'

'So there would've been a balance payable?'

'Seems as if that was one of the things that was putting Ned Molland off buying,' said Harpe, who had obviously been pretty diligent in his way. 'All White'll get now, of course, will be the insurance money.'

'And his debt rubbed out,' murmured Sloan reflectively, 'if it was a gaming one.'

'Must say I hadn't thought of that,' admitted Harpe.

'Brake cable didn't fail?' asked Sloan, though he knew Happy Harry would have checked on that too.

'No.' Harpe frowned.

'Why did White leave the engine ticking over and the gear shift in drive?' asked Sloan. 'Sounds dangerous to me.'

'Oh, you can do that with an automatic. No problem.'

'Well, there was this time, from the sound of it. Why did he do it, anyway?'

'Like I said, I think he just wanted to impress on Ned Molland how quiet the engine was.'

'And instead,' remarked Sloan, 'he seems to have impressed the engine on him, poor fellow. Well, Harry, put me out of my misery. If it wasn't the brakes, what was it then? Mice?'

'I don't think it was mice, Sloan,' said Inspector Harpe seriously. 'I think it was just old age and bad luck.'

95

'What was?'

'The hose connecting the manifold to the brake servo breaking just when it did. It's rubber and I should say that it was pretty badly perished to start with.' Harry drained his tea and said lugubriously: 'Only to be expected in a car of that date, of course, though there was a patch of oil on it too and that always accelerates perishing. All it needed was the vibration from the engine running for a bit to fracture it completely.'

'Then what?' Sloan held up a hand: 'But spare me too many technicalities, Harry.'

'When that hose breaks you lose your vacuum,' said Happy Harry simply.

'And we all know that Nature abhors a vacuum,' said Sloan patiently. 'So what happens next?'

'You get a sudden inrush of air into the manifold.'

'And?' said Sloan, draining his cup.

'And that would cause the engine to speed up momentarily.'

'Would it, indeed?' said Sloan thoughtfully.

'And that,' continued Harpe, 'would bring the torque converter into operation.'

'So?'

'So the car would leap forward before the engine died.'

'The creditor it was who died,' murmured Sloan almost to himself.

'I reckon that White was dead lucky not to have got killed, too,' said Inspector Harpe. 'If he hadn't been standing where he was, to one side, he would have been. More tea?'

'Thanks,' replied Sloan abstractedly. 'Harry, what about the rest of the engine? Did you find anything wrong at all?'

'Not a thing. I went over the inside, too.' He sighed. 'I checked the dashboard. Lovely piece of work . . .'

'What is?' said Sloan, his mind elsewhere.

'The dashboard. Polished walnut. You don't see that sort of thing any more these days.' He sighed again. 'I'd quite forgotten how good real leather smells.' Inspector Harpe got to his feet. 'Another round of sandwiches, too? Ham, wasn't it?'

'No, thanks. Just the tea.' Sloan sat and stared unseeingly round the police canteen, his mind elsewhere, until Inspector Harpe came back.

'One tea, no sugar, coming up . . .'

'Harry, that was no accident last night.'

'What?' said Harry, lowering his cup without drinking anything. 'Sloan, are you saying that . . .'

'I am suggesting that the car might have a lovely smell but that the accident has a very nasty one.' He leaned forward. 'Listen, Harry, suppose this man Daniel White created just the right degree of perishing in the vacuum pipe himself and knew that the vibration caused by letting the engine run for a little while would mean that sooner or later it would be bound to fracture . . .'

'Having carefully placed his victim in front of and slightly below the car before it shot forward,' contributed the Traffic man intelligently.

Sloan nodded. You could say this for old Harry: he wasn't slow to cotton on. 'And having set things up so that he wasn't in the car himself . . .'

'Neat, I call it,' said Harpe appreciatively.

'All White had to do,' said Sloan, 'was to stand well back himself and he's in the clear in both senses. How to lose a creditor and collect on the insurance in – er – one fell swoop.' He drained his tea. 'I'd say you were dealing with murder, Harry.'

'Oh, no, I'm not,' said Inspector Harpe vigorously. 'You are, Sloan. It's not my department. I'm Traffic, remember?'

One Under the Eight

'AH, SLOAN, there you are.' The Assistant Chief Constable looked up from behind a very large desk indeed. 'Come along in.'

'Thank you, sir,' said Sloan warily. He had no idea why he had been summoned so suddenly to this august presence. It couldn't be for a breach of discipline because in that case the rules and regulations called for him to have had a rousting from his own Superintendent first and he hadn't.

'And take a seat.'

'Thank you, sir.'

Detective Inspector Sloan didn't relax. Although as far as he knew he hadn't blotted his copy-book, in these post-Sheehy days you never could tell.

'I dare say, Inspector,' the Assistant Chief Constable stroked a lean chin, 'you like to be kept in touch with what's going on in your manor.'

'Naturally, sir.' That was a safe enough thing to say, surely?

The Assistant Chief Constable steepled his long bony fingers. 'It's rather a delicate matter.'

'I understand, sir.' And Sloan thought that he did. The Assistant Chief Constable was unusual in that as well as being a university graduate, he was unmistakably a member of Calleshire's upper crust of County families. Well connected, it was called. It wouldn't be altogether surprising, then, if one of Calleshire's *gratin* did have a serious problem, for it to reach first – and quite informally – one of their own.

Sloan cast about rapidly in his mind. There had been no rumour of trouble at Calle Castle and as far as he knew none of the Earl of Ornum's notoriously high-spirited family was in difficulties just now.

'One has to be so careful,' said the ACC vaguely, 'when – er – outside agencies are involved. Protocol and so forth.'

'Quite,' said Sloan. It wasn't the Duke of Calleshire, then.

'Tact and diplomacy, Sloan. That's what we need.'

'Yes, sir.' Or the Earl of Ornum's younger sons.

'And total – er – reliability.'

Sloan made a noncommittal sound far down in his throat. He wasn't pledging himself to a conspiracy to defeat the ends of justice for anybody. Discretion, yes; privilege, no.

'Don't want the Constabulary to be seen putting its oar in too heavily either, of course, even though it's our own bailiwick.'

'No, sir,' said Sloan, still mystified.

'Nothing in writing, naturally.'

'I see, sir.' Now that Sloan came to look properly at the ACC's desk he saw that in fact there was nothing on it.

'Quite a tricky business, actually.'

'What outside agency, exactly, sir?' They'd got a nutter who lived under the railway arches in Berebury who attributed all his difficulties to unnamed 'outside agencies'.

'Good question, Sloan.' He nodded and said 'They were a bit cagey about telling me what they were called.'

'I see, sir.' The chap under the arches at Berebury would never be specific either.

'It's one of these new Intelligence outfits that's a bit wary of saying exactly what it does.'

'Ah,' said Sloan.

'Department K is what we're to call it. Run by someone known only as Troy.'

'A woman?'

'Could be,' agreed the ACC. 'They usually are these days.'

That women were better at Intelligence work was something some male chauvinists found hard to accept. The others merely attributed it to a natural talent to deceive.

'And there's something in my – our – patch, sir, that interests them?' said Sloan in spite of himself.

'There's Sir Paul Markham.'

'Over at Almstone?' Even Sloan had heard of him, distinguished scientists being few and far between in the rural hinterland of the market town of Berebury.

'None other. Clever chap, Sir Paul.'

'So I've heard, sir.'

'Knows a lot about rare metals.'

'Does he, sir?'

The Assistant Chief Constable studied his finger-tips. 'The Ministry of Defence is always interested in rare metals.'

'I can see that they might be, sir.'

'Unfortunately' – the ACC sounded genuinely regretful – 'it would seem that the men from the Ministry so to speak are not the only people interested in rare metals – or, rather more pertinently, in Sir Paul Markham.'

'Who knows all about them?'

'Just so, Inspector. Happily, it would seem that this interest extends not so much to his person . . .'

Sloan nodded. It wasn't a case of murder or abduction that was the problem, then.

'. . . as in the outcome of his latest researches into some element called querremitte.'

'Someone else wants them?'

'Someone else would appear to have got them,' said the ACC cogently.

Sloan thought he began to see where he came in. 'From his house?'

'Yes. That's the interesting thing.' The ACC leaned forward. 'You see, Inspector, this department . . .'

'K?' This was the sort of thing he'd read in comics when he was still at school.

'None other. Only hours before they had rigged his house up with what they thought was a totally secure alarm system.'

'And,' divined Sloan, who thought he now knew why he'd been summoned, 'this department doesn't want anyone to know they've failed?'

'That's one thing.'

'And they want to be allowed to find out why before . . .'

'How and who, actually.'

'. . . their system failed before anyone else does?'

'You've got it in one, Inspector.'

'And you mean, sir, they want to be left alone to find out without our coming into it at all?' Sloan sat back a little. 'On our patch without us, you might say?'

'Precisely,' agreed the ACC. 'And they're just telling us out of courtesy.'

'And,' said Sloan, 'to stop us taking any action on our own part should anything – er – come to our attention?'

'Exactly. Or,' the ACC extended this, 'even should the loss be reported to us by anyone else. I gather Sir Paul is very, very cross.' He paused and then added slowly: 'That's what they want . . . I, on the other hand, would like something else, Inspector.'

'Sir?'

'It'd be a bit of a feather in Calleshire's cap if we could get there ahead of them, wouldn't it?'

'Yes, sir,' agreed Sloan neutrally. He couldn't very well suggest that the ACC must be joking. There was, after all, his pension to think of.

'You see, it wasn't just a simple break-in.'

Sloan would have liked to have asked whether that was good or bad but he held his peace.

The ACC shook his head. 'Oh, no. Department K've got a bigger problem than that in the woodwork. Much bigger.'

'Sir?'

'This security system of theirs – which they'd only just fitted to Sir Paul's house, remember – relied on a code number being programmed into the control panel.'

'They nearly always do.' Sloan thought he was familiar with almost all the devices on the market designed to help the prudent householder try to protect his possessions. Department K, though, probably had a few he didn't know about.

'This number was, at the time of the break-in, known to only three people besides Sir Paul himself.'

'That narrows the field nicely, sir, doesn't it?'

'All of them,' said the ACC impressively, 'members of Department K.'

'What!'

'I thought that would get you, Sloan,' said the ACC with visible satisfaction. 'It did me and it has Department K.'

'But how come . . . sorry, sir . . . I mean in what circumstances was the code passed on?'

'These three from Department K agreed on the number with Sir Paul and programmed the system with it, finishing about six o'clock on Friday afternoon. Sir Paul immediately left by train for Cambridge to do some work in a laboratory there.' The ACC frowned. 'Before eight o'clock that very same evening his house was entered via the front door

using the code number and his research work on querremitte stolen.'

'These people from Department K ... did they go
straight back to London afterwards?'

'That is the interesting thing, Sloan. They stayed in Calleshire. One of them lives here and the other two had
arranged to go back with him for the night . . .'

Detective Sloan dismissed any impure thoughts he might
have had about whether they would still be claiming their
subsistence allowances and said instead: 'I take it they alibi
each other?'

'Yes, but the Department doesn't think it's a conspiracy,
if that's what you mean.' The ACC frowned and went on:
'The chap who told me all this – name of Cumming,
George Cumming – their boss, said they needed to find
out pretty quickly which one of them it was that the
Ancient Mariner had got at.'

'The Ancient Mariner, sir?'

' "He stoppeth one in three",' quoted the ACC. 'There
are three suspects.'

'Yes, sir,' said Sloan dutifully. It all sounded more like
the 'three-card trick' to him – and that was more difficult
to perform than most people thought.

'And,' went on the ACC, 'just to make it all more com-
plicated they want to find out without letting him know
they've found out.'

'I can see that they might, sir.' It was what the police
tried to do with the smaller drug pushers. Identify and
observe.

'Or her, actually. There's a Miss Elland – no oil painting
but brains – and two men.'

'I see, sir.' The other name for the 'three-card trick' was
'Spot the Lady'.

'The man who lives in Calleshire is Andrew Birkby and

the third one is called Farnley – Colin Farnley.' The ACC paused. 'All three left Sir Paul's and went straight back to Birkby's house in the same car. They got a move on because Birkby had previously arranged to hold a wine-tasting at his home in aid of some local good cause. The church roof or some such thing.'

Detective Inspector Sloan nodded. 'I take it that no one stopped to make a telephone call or used a mobile phone while they were alone?'

'The funny thing, Sloan, is that they don't appear to have been alone.' The ACC jerked his head. 'That's bothering George Cumming more than somewhat. It's almost as if one of the three was making quite sure that none of them was in a position to pass on the number.'

'And yet one of them,' pointed out Sloan ineluctably, 'contrived to do so.'

'Oh, yes. The burglary took place thirty miles away while all three of them were in sight of each other and they were the only ones who knew the code number.'

'It could have been agreed beforehand.'

'Sir Paul chose it himself on the spot after they arrived.' The ACC resumed his account. 'They were a little late getting to Birkby's house – the audience was already assembled and waiting, not to say restive – and he was leading the tasting so he went straight to the main table in his drawing-room, fussed about a bit with the bottles that were there and then got cracking.'

Sloan wasn't sure if the ACC had meant to be punny so he didn't say anything.

'Birkby got his bottles out as quickly as he could – the glasses were already set out on the front of the table . . .'

'He didn't change the glasses about, did he, sir?' asked Sloan quickly. 'Rearrange them into groups of – say four and seven – or do anything like that?'

'No, but good thinking, Sloan.'

'How do we know all this, sir?'

'Their immediate superior, this chap George Cumming whom I've been telling you about, was there by invitation. He lives in the next county and he's come over ostensibly for the wine-tasting but actually for a rendezvous with his staff.'

'I see, sir.'

The ACC said: 'He now thinks he was invited so that he, too, could alibi one of them . . .'

'Looks very like it, doesn't it, sir?'

'And he doesn't like it.'

'I don't blame him,' said Sloan immediately. No one liked being made a patsy of but especially, he imagined, not a high-ranking Intelligence officer. 'But somehow or other the secret number was disclosed to someone else in the house . . .'

'In the room, Sloan. Cumming's pretty sure about that.'

'Who must have slipped out for a moment to telephone a confederate, who promptly proceeded to Sir Paul's to do the robbery.'

'Disclosed by one of the three.' The ACC kept to the point at issue with a skill born of much practice with the County Council Police Committee.

'Andrew Birkby, who was running the wine-tasting, or Colin Farnley or Miss Elland who were in the audience . . .'

'In the front row of the audience, Sloan. They had reserved seats and sat with Mrs Birkby. George Cumming was in the row behind them.'

'Which meant they couldn't see anything going on any-where else in the room,' concluded Sloan. He thought for a moment. 'They could have scratched their ears or something, sir.'

'Cumming swears they didn't do anything like that.'

'Something in Birkby's spiel about the wine?' Sloan didn't know a lot about wine but he knew men who waxed lyrical about it with a special, mannered prose all of their own.

'Cumming says there wasn't anything he could spot.' The ACC started to fumble in the pocket of his uniform jacket. 'He even wondered if something could have been made of the names of the wines . . .' He fished out a list.

'Or their years,' suggested Sloan. Good wines had dates, surely, and dates were numbers.

'Well, the cryptographers in Department K didn't have any bright ideas about that, Cumming says, but there's no harm in our trying.' The ACC looked at the list. 'The first one was a 1991 Muscadet de Sevre-et-Maine which George Cumming thought was a good straightforward dry white wine.'

'I suppose the S and M of Sevre-et-Maine could stand for figures,' said Sloan doubtfully.

'The next one was a red – fruity purple was how Cumming described it to me. A 1992 Merlot – Vin du Pays des Coteaux de l'Ardèche . . . ever driven through the Ardèche Gorges, Inspector?'

'No, sir.'

'I gather it's standard practice at wine-tastings to serve a *vin du pays* to encourage the penniless.'

'Really, sir? What came next?'

The ACC studied the list. 'A rosé – to my mind a rosé wine is neither one thing nor the other – as Sir Winston Churchill said so famously about Sir Alfred Bossom. It was a Côtes de Provence 1992 and dry.'

'That's one white, one red and one pink . . .'

'Odd that, now you come to mention it,' said the ACC, frowning. 'You'd have thought he'd have started with the whites and stayed with them instead of going on to a red next. Mind you, as I understand it, Birkby's only an amateur wine buff – doing it for charity and all that – and he might not have known any better.'

Sloan nodded, but didn't comment.

'Then it was back to a white wine,' continued the ACC, the list still in his hand. 'A Sauvignon de Touraine 1992. Actually, now I come to think of it, the number we're looking for couldn't have been the sum of the years of the wine because he – if it was he – couldn't have known in advance what they added up to.'

'Very true, sir.'

'Number five was another rosé – Domaine de Limbardie. I don't care what you say about them – sweet, fruity and a suspicion of raspberry was what Cumming said – I still think you're wasting your time drinking them.'

'Yes, sir.' There was a lot to be said for beer.

'The last one was a full-blooded red – strong vigorous flavour and all that. A Côtes de Ventoux 1990.'

'That's another white, a rosé and a red, then, in that order . . . that all, sir?'

The ACC said: 'I asked Cumming that. He said there was one other wine – a white that Birkby poured out into half a dozen glasses as soon as he got to the table but that he didn't talk about it. Cumming didn't know what it was and never did find out because he wasn't given a taste of that one.'

There was a silence.

Presently the ACC said lightly: 'Now, if it had been port we could have said it was a two-pipe problem . . .'

'Would I be right, sir, in saying that the only thing that strikes you as at all unusual about this list is the order in which the wines were presented for tasting?'

'Well, it's not the batting order I would have chosen myself, Inspector,' agreed the ACC amiably enough. 'I'd have put out the two whites first, the two rosés after them

– except that I'd have left them out in the first place – and then the two reds last. Stands to reason, doesn't it?'

'Yes,' said Sloan quietly. 'So, I'm pretty sure, sir, that that's where the answer must be, though I don't know what it is.'

'Start with the light whites and work your way up to the heavy reds. That would have been the right thing to do.'

'The right thing in the wrong order,' mused Sloan, half aloud. 'It must mean something.'

'But what, Inspector? What?'

'Ah, sir, there you have me. We don't know what the colours represent so we can't begin to work anything out . . .' He stopped in mid-sentence. 'You can express numbers just using 0 and 1 in binary arithmetic, sir, because they do it for computers that way.'

'I believe you, Inspector.' The ACC winced visibly. The Constabulary's computer was known throughout the Force to be anathema to the ACC. It had taken the blame for every mistake made by Headquarters ever since it had been installed.

'You could have had the red standing for one and the white for nought . . .'

'That still leaves the rosé . . .'

'And it doesn't get us anywhere . . .' Sloan scribbled a row of numbers in his notebook before showing it to the ACC.

'32, 16, 8, 4, 2, 1, Sloan? What do they mean?'

'That if you put a nought or a one under them and add up the figures with a one underneath it, you can show a total.'

The ACC looked somewhat sceptical.

'Look, sir,' said Sloan persuasively, retrieving his notebook, 'if I put a one under the 32 and the 8 and the 2 and noughts under the other figures I can say it represents 42.'

'Can you?'

'You just add 32, 8 and 2 and ignore the 16, 4 and 1. But it doesn't help us now.'

'No?'

'If I know anything about security systems, sir, it'll be a four-figure number they've programmed in, and one that doesn't begin with a one.'

'Nice idea, though. The red for a one and – say – the white for a nought. It still leaves the rosé, though . . .'

'Say that again!' Sloan remembered just in time that he was speaking to a very superior officer. 'I mean, would you mind repeating that, please, sir?'

'That still leaves the rosé . . .'

'Suppose it was all to the power of three, sir, instead of two? Not binary arithmetic but ternary.'

'You've lost me, Inspector,' said the ACC with disarming honesty.

'Suppose the numbers were 243, 81, 27, 9, 3 and 1. What would that give us?'

The ACC stared at the list of wines. 'The first – the first, that is, from the speaker's left to right, Cumming's right to left – was a white . . .'

'We'll call white nought.'

'The next was a red – a Merlot.'

'If that's three then we'd pick up six there . . .'

'Would we?' The ACC looked exceedingly doubtful. 'Then there was a rosé.'

'We'll say rosé stands for the number one. That comes under the figure 9 so we can add one nine to the six we've got already, making fifteen,' said Sloan rapidly warming to the idea. 'The next one was another white, wasn't it, sir?'

'The Sauvignon.'

'We can ignore that, then, because white means nought.'

'Then another rosé.'

'One under the figure 81. Eighty-one and fifteen brings

us to ninety-six. The last one was a red, wasn't it?'

'A Côtes de Ventoux. Ever been up Mont Ventoux, Inspector?'

'No, sir.' Sloan felt that it was other – even dizzier – heights that he was scaling just at the moment. 'The unit for that would be 243 and red means two so that is twice 243 which is 486 plus the 96 we'd got to already.'

'If you say so, Inspector.'

Suddenly downcast, Sloan sank back on his chair in disappointment. 'But that still only comes to 582 which isn't a four-figure number. It won't do. Sorry, sir . . . it was just an idea.'

'Aren't you forgetting something, Sloan?' The ACC gave him a quizzical look.

'Sir?'

'There was another wine on the table.'

'But Mr Cumming didn't taste that, sir.'

'The first thing Birkby did when he got to the wines was pour out six glasses of one of them – even though he was late in getting started. Doesn't that strike you as rather odd?'

'I hadn't thought of that.'

'And all Birkby did with it at that stage was leave the empty bottle standing on the table.' The ACC looked positively cheerful now.

'I still don't see . . .' Then Sloan slapped his thigh. 'Of course, sir! An empty bottle at the end.' He looked a good deal more respectfully at the ACC who wasn't nearly as innumerate – nor as much of a figurehead – as he might have been forgiven for thinking. 'An empty bottle. It's so simple . . .'

'Representing a nought at the end of the number,' said the ACC, pardonably pleased with himself.

'That was really clever,' said Sloan generously.

'But not clever enough,' said the ACC, reaching for his telephone and dialling a London number. 'Department K? Put me through to Mr George Cumming, would you, please? Thank you.' There was only the slightest of delays and then the ACC said: 'Calleshire Constabulary here. About your little problem, Mr Cumming ... the one you were telling me about. Have you solved it yet? No?'

The ACC grinned and reached his hand out across his desk for Sloan's notebook. He squinted down at it and said down the wire: 'Would the number of the Professor's security system have been 5820, by any chance? It would? Ah! Then I think we may be able to tell you who your defector is and – er – how he did it.' He cocked his head into an alert listening position. There was a pause. Then the ACC said: 'What's that? Oh, no trouble at all. One of my men was on to it straight away. A message in a bottle, I think you might say ...'

Bare Essentials

'NASTY,' observed Dr Dabbe.

Detective Inspector C. D. Sloan couldn't have agreed with him more. There was something very unattractive indeed about the dead body they were both contemplating.

'Very nasty,' said Dr Dabbe, moving his stance slightly the better to conduct his external examination of the deceased *in situ.*

Sloan nodded. He didn't know whether the pathologist was referring to the woman or the manner of her death but neither was appealing in any way. The dead woman was quite naked and had been decidedly corpulent, not to say obese.

Both these last two factors undoubtedly had some relevance to her having been found where she was now – lying in the Hot Room in Berebury's local health farm. What the connection – if any – was with her death was something on which both the pathologist and Detective Inspector Sloan were presently working.

'I should say she's been roasted alive,' pronounced Dabbe tersely.

'Roasted, doctor?' Sloan was startled into actually doubting the pathologist, something he'd never ever done before.

'Not scalded or burnt,' said Dr Dabbe succinctly, 'and, like a lobster, alive.'

The comparison with a lobster, thought Sloan, was relevant enough. The body was an unhappy shade of shiny red.

'Kebabbed,' said the doctor more succinctly still. 'God knows what the temperature in here got up to.'

'It's normal enough now,' remarked Sloan. 'Warm, but not excessively so.' Indeed, an indicator on the wall by the door was set at 'medium heat' and seemed to be accurate enough. Checking out that mechanism would be high on a list of things to be done following this death.

'You can take it from me,' said Dabbe, 'that it wasn't anything like normal a couple of hours or so ago. Although, Sloan,' he added swiftly, 'I can't tell you people exactly when she died. Not yet.'

Detective Inspector Sloan averted his gaze from the body of the dead woman. The temperature must have been off the top of the thermometer to leave her looking like this.

'I should say,' said the pathologist with the lack of emotion of all his ilk, 'that the supply of steam in here turned to dry heat and Bob's your uncle.'

Sloan looked down at a series of pipes running along above the skirting board. 'That would have done it, would it?' he murmured thoughtfully.

The pathologist jerked his head in assent. 'The human body can take a much higher steam heat than it can dry heat. Any Turkish bath attendant could tell you that. The name of this game, Sloan, is thermal shock.'

'Could she have been unconscious first, doctor?' asked Sloan. 'There must have been some reason why she didn't just walk out of here when it started to get too hot.'

'She tried,' said Dr Dabbe. 'Look at her fingernails. See where she had been clawing at something?'

'The door wasn't locked when we arrived,' said Sloan carefully, 'though the key was in the lock.'

'That's as may be, Sloan. Not my province, that.' He frowned. 'All I can say is that there might have been some physical reason why she couldn't get out but I shan't be able to tell you that until after the post-mortem.'

'She could have shouted.'

'Not for long,' said Dabbe chillingly. 'This show was over long before the fat lady sang.' He straightened up. 'Who is she, anyway?'

'A Mrs Bessie Culshaw. According to the manager of this outfit – who's called Graham Pattman, by the way – she and her husband are long-time regulars here. Been coming for years, the manager said. The husband comes here for the golf and she comes here to try to lose weight.'

'Not her life,' said Dr Dabbe absently. He was squinting at the soles of the dead woman's feet.

'The manager's wringing his hands in the hall,' said Sloan. 'A death like this isn't going to do this place any good.'

'I can't tell you whether it's an accident or murder,' said Dabbe, answering Sloan's unspoken question. 'Only the cause of death.'

'And the husband's waiting in one of the quiet rooms with his head in his hands,' continued Sloan. 'I've left my constable sitting with him. He's taking down a statement from him now.'

'You'll have mine when I've done the post-mortem,' said Dr Dabbe briskly, 'but in the mean time I can tell you that she died from the effects of a temperature too high to be compatible with human life.'

The manager's choice of words was nothing like so well ordered or cogent.

'I can't imagine what can possibly have happened, Inspector,' he said, distractedly. 'Or why poor Mrs Culshaw didn't just walk out of the Hot Room. Janice is quite sure the door wasn't locked when she went in to tidy up and found her.'

'Although the key was in the lock,' said Sloan again. That was important.

Pattman wasn't paying attention. 'We've been using that Hot Room ever since we opened and we've never had any trouble there before.'

It was a refrain which Detective Inspector Sloan had heard many times in his daily round. Battle, murder, sudden death, accident and sundry other Jovian thunderbolts had seldom struck ordinary people before in most of the situations that came his – and their – way. Hard as it seemed, all that that meant in practical police terms was that those concerned had had no previous experience in confronting disaster.

That, he decided, listening to the manager now, could be both good and bad.

'I just can't think of anything that could possibly have gone wrong either . . .' said Pattman, his natural volubility made worse by stress.

'Tell me about the Hot Room,' said Sloan.

'It's where clients – patients – go to – er – perspire a lot from the steam heat,' he said, mopping his own brow. 'After having a massage and so forth. Perspiring is the quickest way of losing weight, although,' he added honestly, 'it comes back again as soon as you drink.'

What was it that Sloan had heard that process called? The rhythm method of girth control, that was it.

'Then,' swallowed Pattman, 'they'd go and have a swim in the tepid pool and end up feeling fine.'

Sloan nodded. It sounded to him a perfectly harmless way of spending the morning if you hadn't anything better to do. Anything better to do except eat, of course.

'It's quite terrible, Inspector. Quite terrible. I don't know what will happen now.' The manager's shoulders drooped as a vision of how much less than fine Mrs Culshaw

115

must have been feeling in the Hot Room before she died clearly swam into his mind.

'No.' Sloan could offer no comfort and didn't try. He couldn't decide whether a verdict of murder or accident would do the more harm to the health farm. There probably wasn't much to choose between the effect of the two evils. What mattered to them would be a third evil – bad publicity. 'And I can't help you at this stage.'

'There'll have to be an inquest, of course, won't there . . . ?' The manager's shoulders sagged even further when he contemplated the damage that news of this death would do to the health farm.

'And a police investigation,' said Sloan, adding firmly: 'First, we shall need to find out exactly how Mrs Culshaw died.' The police would want to know why she had died, too, but that would come later. 'It would seem that for an unknown length of time the inlet pipe delivered hot air instead of steam to the Hot Room.'

'Mike – that's our resident maintenance man – is quite adamant that there's never been any trouble in the hot-water system before,' said the manager, a last-ditcher by nature. 'I've got him waiting in my room now, like you said, Inspector.'

'I'll see him as soon as I've had a word with the husband,' said Sloan.

Mr William Culshaw lifted a drawn, anxious face when the Detective Inspector entered the lounge where he had been giving his statement to Detective Constable Crosby.

'Poor Bessie,' he said. 'And all she wanted to do was to be able to tell me she'd lost a few pounds. She always liked it here, you know, Inspector. We've been coming for years. It's – well – restful.'

'I'll need to know about this morning, sir,' said Sloan.

'Of course' said the husband, readily enough. 'We had

breakfast together as usual in our room. My wife wasn't a big breakfast eater – sometimes they'd say that was bad for dieters and sometimes they'd say it was good. If you were to ask me, Inspector, I'd say they didn't know . . .'

Detective Inspector Sloan was an English breakfast man himself but didn't think this was the moment to say so.

'They all knew, all right, Inspector, how she came to be overweight . . .'

It was interesting, noted Sloan, how no one here seemed to use the word 'fat'.

'Oh, yes,' said William Culshaw bitterly. 'Bessie never had a chance of being anywhere near normal weight.'

'How was that, sir?'

'Barclays' Biscuits,' he said.

'Barclays' Biscuits, sir?' Sloan knew Barclays' Biscuits, of course. Who didn't? Their packet with the picture of the happy, plump little girl eating one on it was part of the national culture and had been for years . . . Light dawned. He said: 'She wasn't . . . ?'

'She was,' he said, nodding vigorously. 'Little Miss Barclay. She was always being photographed eating one of Barclays' Famous Biscuits when she was small. She liked the Bourbon ones best . . .'

'With the chocolate cream,' endorsed Sloan, back to his own childhood in an instant. He could conjure up the taste even now . . .

'You can work out what happened,' said William Culshaw with a certain melancholy. 'A moment on the lips and a lifetime on the hips. And they always say a fat child is a fat adult.'

'Yes,' said Sloan. His own theory was that it was the sweetness of the apple not the attractions of Eve that had led to the downfall of mankind in the Garden of Eden. This didn't seem to be the moment to advance that either.

Instead he said: 'You were telling me about this morning, sir . . .'

William Culshaw said: 'After breakfast, I left Bessie and her friend, Eileen Smith . . .'

'Eileen Smith?' said Sloan sharply. 'Was she in the Hot Room, too?'

'No,' said Bessie's husband, 'but I thought she would be. She and my wife always booked the time there together. Seems she was called away. That's what Graham Pattman told me' – his face crinkled – 'afterwards.'

Sloan made a note. 'Go on . . .'

'I did what I usually do – collected my clubs and walked over to the golf course.'

'And what sort of time would that have been, sir?'

'I should say about half-past nine, give or take ten minutes . . .'

Dr Dabbe had given it as his considered professional opinion that something measurable in minutes at a high temperature would have been long enough to kill Bessie Culshaw.

'And then?'

'I played a round with the husband of another resident here – Stanley Cox – and then came back here in time for luncheon.'

'Were you,' asked Sloan delicately, 'expecting to have this with your wife?'

William Culshaw, whom Sloan's mother would have described as thin as a darning needle sideways, shook his head. 'Bessie had to have her meal in the Salad Room with the others on light meals.'

That made sense to Sloan. Exciting the gustatory senses of the starving by the sight of a square meal didn't make any sense at all: especially for this Jack Spratt and his wife.

Culshaw said: 'There is what you might call a normal

dining-room here, too, for non-patients and those who have been – er – very good.'

Detective Inspector Sloan ignored the moral overtones implicit in the statement and enquired instead when William Culshaw had got back from the golf course.

'It must have been something after twelve, Inspector. I put my clubs away and went into the bar for a drink with Cox before we ate.'

'When would you have expected to see your wife again?'

'Tea-time,' he said promptly. 'She needed her rest in the afternoon.' His face clouded. 'Otherwise I'd have gone looking for her myself.'

Janice, the staff member who had found Bessie Culshaw when she had gone in to tidy the Hot Room, was still in shock but Sloan did not say so. Instead he went back to the manager's room and saw Mike, the maintenance man. He was very glad, when he did, that the first thing he had done when he got to the health farm was to have had the man pinned down in his office by the manager in much the same way as Detective Constable Crosby was making quite sure William Culshaw didn't leave the Residents' Lounge.

As soon as the fellow started talking it was clear that he had one object in view and one only – that of minding his own back.

'Never had no complaints from anyone this morning about no water,' Mike said belligerently, his arms folded tightly across his chest. 'Nobody reported nothing, not to me. And them lot in the kitchen'd've shouted pretty quick, too, I can tell you if they hadn't had anything to wash their fancy vegetables in.'

'Here at the Health Farm,' said Graham Pattman, in an agony of concern about putting up a good public relations front, 'we try to compensate for a shortage of – er –

substance – in the diet with an emphasis on the first-class presentation of – er – such food as is allow— recommended.'

'Moreover,' said Mike with the confidence of one who knows, 'the house stop-cock's under the kitchen sink so no one can have got at that without them lot in there noticing for all that they're mostly foreigners.'

'Jacques, our head chef,' intervened the manager swiftly, 'has an international reputation for this sort of cuisine.'

'And the outside stop-cock where the water main comes in?' said Detective Inspector Sloan, house-owner himself.

'A Sabbath day's march down the drive near the front gate and I haven't had a chance to look at that yet,' said Mike, aggrieved. 'Not what with being put in here and told not to move.'

Sloan remained unmoved.

'First thing I know about anything's being up the creek's when Mr Pattman here sent for me,' he said. 'Just before you lot got here, and I haven't been able to look at anything yet, have I?'

'Then we'll do it now,' said Sloan. Crosby could carry on keeping an eye on the deceased's husband.

'It's under some bushes. . .'

'Before we go out there,' said Sloan, 'you can show me where the water supply to the Hot Room comes from . . .'

Mike led the way back past the Hot Room, now occupied by two fingerprint experts and a Scenes of Crime Officer, and into the adjoining room. It was a combined flower room and cloakroom – a relict of the days in which the health farm had been a large country house. A couple of golf trolleys were parked against the further wall and a pile of suitcases stood in front of another. There was a deep sink and a large draining-board on which stood an electric kettle and an empty mug.

'You can see where the pipes come through the wall and run along above the wainscot,' said Mike, stooping and tapping the woodwork, 'and then through this wall and into the old morning-room.'

'That's where our masseuse works,' said Pattman. 'Mrs Culshaw had had her massage before she went into the Hot Room.'

Detective Inspector Sloan bent down to examine the water pipes. He had to move the two golf trolleys out from the wall – one, the electric one, was quite heavy, a large battery contrivance sitting on its cross-bar – to see the entire length of the pipes. To the naked eye they looked undamaged. There was no sign of a water leak either in that room or the next – or indeed in any of the rooms which the pipes traversed on their way round the building from the boiler-room. Nor was there any form of additional stop-cock between the boiler-room and the health farm's Hot Room.

'What did I say?' demanded Mike triumphantly. 'Nothing wrong with the system, like I said.'

Sloan's personal radio crackled. 'Now we'll go outside,' he said, after listening to the message.

The three of them made an unlikely trio as they trooped down the drive of the health farm. Waiting for them at the entrance gate were the two Berebury Police photographers, Williams and Dyson.

'Mike here,' announced Sloan, 'is going to show us by pointing exactly where the outside stop-cock is. He is not,' added Sloan meaningfully, 'going to move off the path while he does so.'

'If you was to look to the left of that post over there,' offered Mike, 'and scrape the leaves away I reckon you'd find a little metal cover.'

The cameras clicked and then very cautiously Sloan

advanced through the carpet of last year's beech leaves which covered all the ground in sight.

'A "Babes in the Wood" job is it, then, Inspector?' said Williams, the senior photographer.

'No,' said Sloan shortly. 'We're looking for evidence that some person or persons unknown turned this stop-cock off for a short time this morning.' That it would have been almost certainly at the same time as the same person or persons saw fit to turn the key in the lock of the Hot Room door he saw no reason to say.

The camera clicked again and then very, very carefully Sloan started to clear away the natural debris of several seasons to expose an iron plate. It was just where Mike had said it would be. It couldn't have been called a manhole because it was only big enough to take an arm.

The photographers took shots of the undisturbed leaves before Sloan indicated that they could advance on the stop-cock.

'I don't check it all that often,' said Mike, 'seeing as how there's never been any trouble in that department.'

The detritus round the metal cover would seem to Sloan's gardener's eye to have drifted there rather than been arranged over it. It was therefore no surprise to him, when the metal cover had been prised open, to see no sign of human interference.

'Reckon what you want, Inspector,' said Williams, the photographer and the humorist of the party, as a pair of centipedes and a leatherjacket scuttled away from the sudden light, 'is one of those forensic entomologists. I dare say they could tell you when this was last opened up by counting their legs.'

'If you were to ask me,' chimed in Dyson, 'I should say not since the old Queen died.'

'I shan't ask you,' said Detective Inspector Sloan tartly,

122

'but remember that defence counsel might.'

It was Graham Pattman who blanched. 'It must have been an accident,' he said. 'A most unfortunate accident . . .'

Detective Inspector Sloan said nothing. True accidents were the province of other people – Coroners, of course; the Press, naturally; the public utilities, sometimes; insurance companies and their assessors, usually but not – definitely not – the police. If Mrs Bessie Culshaw's death was an accident then he could pack up here and now and go back to the Police Station.

But he was beginning to be sure it wasn't. And he had already put a man on to establishing exactly how the victim's intended companion in the Hot Room – Eileen Smith – had come to be called away when she had been.

He left the group and walked across the ample grounds towards the golf course.

'Staying here must cost a bomb,' he remarked to the young golf professional when he got there.

'It does,' said the young man simply. 'And if the fat ones played they could get thin for nothing but it doesn't seem to work like that.'

Sloan asked him when Mr Cox and Mr Culshaw had gone out and come in that morning.

' 'Bout half nine, Inspector, and they must have got back something round about twelve. It's not a long course,' he said a trifle defensively, 'seeing how it was designed for the older man.'

'You'd need to be rich to come here,' agreed Sloan, tacitly acknowledging that as a rule money and age marched hand in hand more often than did wealth and youth.

The young man wasn't as discreet as the manager. 'From what I heard she had the money,' he said. 'Just as well because his firm had folded. It was in the papers. They

123

don't get a lot of young people up at the farm,' admitted the professional.

'So you don't get many good games,' said Sloan. Age and corpulence went together too, more often than not.

'I wouldn't say that,' murmured the golf pro. 'I go round with some of the oldies myself sometimes if they haven't got a partner.'

'And knock spots off them, I suppose?'

The young man shook his head. 'Not if I can help it, but it's not always as easy as that. Some of these old boys may not hit a long ball but they're deadly round the green.'

'And they don't always have to lug their trolleys round with them,' he said. 'Which of the two,' he asked idly, 'had the electric trolley?' William Culshaw had looked a fit man to him – he had yet to interview Stanley Cox.

The professional frowned. 'Neither. Not if you're talking about Mr Culshaw and Mr Cox.'

'I am.'

'Then they don't have electric trolleys,' said the professional firmly. 'Either of them. They went round this morning without and I know because I was behind them all the way round.'

Sloan stiffened. 'Don't leave here until I come back . . .'

He went straight back to the health farm and into the old flower room. The two golf trolleys were still there, one with its battery contrivance on the cross shaft. He bent down to examine it. It certainly comprised electrical equipment of some sort. Two leads came out of it, one now clamped to each leg of the golf trolley.

He straightened up and started to think hard.

At a guess the two leads could have reached the water pipe above the skirting board – but something was beginning to make him think they had. He'd need a magnifying lens to know for sure if they'd ever been clamped to the pipes instead of the golf trolley legs – not that this told him anything.

Yet.

Nor did the name plate on the equipment, which was German.

He stood there alone for a long minute and thought hard. There was something stirring in his memory – something to do with his brother-in-law's house. That was it. That house had been a real jerry-built affair of bodged workmanship and they'd thought they'd have big trouble when they'd needed to drain the hot-water system. There hadn't been a drain tap, that was what had worried his brother-in-law, not a mechanical man.

It hadn't fazed the plumber one little bit.

No, he'd come along with a big box of tricks, plugged into the electricity, cut through the pipe and put a drain tap in the hot-water system without losing a drop of water. 'Behold, the iceman cometh,' was how his brother-in-law had described it.

Detective Inspector Sloan left the flower room and went back to the lounge where William Culshaw was having his statement read over to him by Detective Constable Crosby.

'Just a few more questions, sir,' said Sloan at his smoothest. 'Can you just tell me again what you did when you got back from the golf course?'

'Had a bit of a wash and brush up,' said Culshaw, 'put on a tie and so forth – they're quite particular here – and went along to the bar to have a drink with Stanley Cox.'

'And then?'

'Went into luncheon with him.'

'Did you go back to the flower room before you went to eat?'

'I did,' said Culshaw, nodding. 'I thought I might have dropped my pen there and I had.'

'I think,' said Detective Inspector Sloan coldly, 'that you went back to the flower room to remove two connecting leads from the hot-water pipe leading to the Hot Room and to unlock the door of the Hot Room which you had locked as you came in from your round of golf.'

The colour of Culshaw's face told a tale all of its own, incapable of subterfuge by its possessor.

'You had applied these when you came in from golf,' said Sloan, 'and while you were having a drink the apparatus refrigerated the water in the pipe causing it to freeze and block the pipe . . .'

The man's colour had gone from grey to putty.

'Thus cutting off the water supply,' continued Sloan, unmoved, 'from which the steam for the Hot Room was made for about twenty minutes.'

And from putty colour to paper white.

'Which,' said Sloan, making a sign to Detective Constable Crosby, 'was long enough to bring about the death of your wife.'

Home is the Hunter

'EVER HAD ANYTHING to do with an Extradition Order, Sloan?' asked Police Superintendent Leeyes.

'No, sir,' said Detective Inspector Sloan warily.

'Now's your chance, then,' said Leeyes.

'Sir?'

'It's never too late to learn,' said Leeyes. 'All the good books say so.'

'Yes, sir,' said Sloan, since this was very true.

The Superintendent consulted a piece of paper on his desk. 'It's from France.'

'A friendly power.'

The Superintendent, suspecting irony, ignored this. 'A Madame Vercollas of 17 rue de la Pierre Blanche, St-Amand d'Huiss ... Huisse ...' Leeyes gave up the unequal struggle to pronounce Huisselot. 'Anyway she's here in Berebury now, which is all that matters to us.'

'Keeps it simple,' agreed Sloan.

'Nothing like your own patch.' The Superintendent's xenophobia was well known to embrace the next county to Calleshire as well as the next country to England. He had always been one to equate stranger with enemy.

'And the French would like her back, would they, sir?' asked Sloan, getting out his notebook.

'They would,' growled Leeyes. He pushed the Extradition Order from the Home Office across the desk. 'She's wanted on a charge of murdering her husband, Louis Ver-collas, at a place called Corbeaux last September.'

Sloan picked up the paper. 'I take it, sir, that the fine detail isn't anything to do with us.'

'Not really,' said the Superintendent, a trifle wistfully. He always liked to have a finger in any pie that was going.

'Just a matter of handing her over to the French, then?'

'That's all. The Home Office has agreed to her extradition.' Leeyes sounded regretful at this. It went against the grain with him for the British to co-operate with any foreign power, but especially with the French. The Superintendent blamed metrication entirely on Napoleon Bona-parte. 'It should be all quite straightforward . . .'

'Does she speak English?'

'She is English,' said Leeyes. 'It's her husband who was French.'

'I see, sir.'

'And Sloan . . .'

'Sir?'

'You might as well take Crosby with you. It'll get him off my back for the afternoon.'

If possible, Detective Constable Crosby was even more insular than the Superintendent. 'Do we have to deport her ourselves?' he asked as they drove down Berebury High Street.

'She's not being deported,' explained Sloan patiently. 'Deportation's when we're kicking someone out of the country. Extradition's when they're being asked for by another country with which we have a treaty.'

'*Vive la difference!*' said the Constable, changing gear.

In due course the police car reached a neat semi-detached house in a quiet street in a residential area of the town. The doorbell was answered by a pleasant-faced, middle-aged woman.

'Madame Vercollas?' began Sloan.

The woman shook her head. 'That's my sister. I'm Anne Pickford. Come in and I'll get her for you.' She led the way into the sitting-room, calling out: 'Laura, someone to see you! Can you come?'

Madame Vercollas was a younger edition of the woman who had answered the door. 'Good afternoon . . .'

Sloan explained the nature of their errand. Laura Vercollas sat down rather suddenly in one of the armchairs. Her sister murmured something about a cup of tea and retreated to the kitchen.

'I'm sorry to be silly, Inspector,' said Laura Vercollas wanly. 'I ought to have known why you had come. My notary in Huisselot warned me to expect all this.'

'Quite so.'

'But he didn't know how long the formalities would take.'

Sloan cleared his throat. 'Well, the due processes of law have been gone through now and I must warn you that . . .'

'Yes, yes,' she interrupted quickly. 'I do understand the procedure.' She twisted her lips into an awkward smile. 'In a way, Inspector, it's a relief that you've come and the waiting's over.'

He nodded with suitable gravity. Just as sometimes it was better to travel hopefully than to arrive, sometimes it was a relief when the axe fell . . . He pulled himself together, glad he hadn't spoken aloud. He wasn't at all sure if they still used the guillotine across the Channel.

'At least,' said Madame Vercollas stoutly, 'I shall have a chance to tell the court that I didn't kill my husband, in spite of what they say.'

'Can you prove it, though?' asked Detective Constable Crosby with interest.

She turned her gaze in his direction. 'I don't know. My

husband was – well – rather older than I, and not a well man. He died in a strange hotel from a massive dose of a narcotic, and the French police say that I gave it to him.'

'Tea,' said Anne Pickford, coming into the room with a tray and dispelling any lingering doubts that Sloan might have had that both sisters were English.

'And you say you didn't poison him,' said Crosby, leaning forward with the air of one trying to get something clear.

Madame Vercollas nodded gently. 'I didn't kill Louis.'

'The evidence . . .' began Crosby, to whom the arm's-length nature of an Extradition Order had not been explained.

'Is all against me,' she said at once.

'Now, now, Laura,' said her sister, 'you mustn't be defeatist.'

Detective Inspector Sloan, who prized realism for its own sake, hitched his shoulders forward and said: 'You understand, madam, that it is the French authorities who . . .'

'I understand all right,' she said calmly, 'and I don't blame them for thinking as they do. For one thing, we were strangers in Corbeaux. I'd never even seen the place before.'

'How did you come to be there?' asked Sloan.

'We were staying in a resort about twenty miles away – Louis thought a holiday might do him good – when suddenly something or somebody there upset Louis and he insisted on leaving the hotel there and then and finding somewhere else that very night.' She hesitated. 'He was like that.'

'A difficult man,' pronounced Anne Pickford judiciously.

Laura Vercollas didn't deny this. She said, 'That's something else they're holding against me: that he wasn't easy to live with . . .'

'And you just happened on Corbeaux?' asked Sloan, interested in spite of himself.

'Louis pointed to the map and said: "We'll try there." '

'He drove?'

'I drove and he directed me,' she said. 'It was practically dark by the time we arrived but he must have had a map because he steered me through the town all right – except for a one-way street that I had to reverse out of. He told me when to stop and I found we were outside the Hôtel Coq d'Or in the Place Dr Jacques Colliard.'

'He went in?'

'I went in, Inspector. Louis didn't move about more than he had to. Not since his last illness. He told me to book a room for five nights, and so I did.'

'Why five?'

'I don't know. But in the end, oddly enough, I was there for the five.'

'You had dinner there?'

She twisted her lips wryly. 'That's something else the police are holding against me. I think they think I'm another Madame de Brinvilliers. Louis wanted to have dinner in our room so they brought it up. We ate alone. You can see how their minds work, can't you?'

'More tea?' asked Anne Pickford.

Laura Vercollas was not diverted. 'Corbeaux is one of those *bastide* towns with a war memorial and fountain in the middle of the square. We had our meal looking out on to the Place. It was lit up and rather nice. And in the morning when I woke up Louis was dead in bed.'

'Had you had snails?' enquired Crosby, who could not have been described as exactly Francophile. 'Or frogs' legs?'

The ghost of a smile crossed her face. '*Potage* and *bœuf bourgugnon*. Nothing likely to upset anyone.' She paused. 'Louis had been ill – I think I told you – and he was always careful what he had in the evening in case it kept him awake. He slept badly enough anyway and he had a lot of nightmares when he did get to sleep. He often used to call out for the doctor in the night, but it was in his sleep. He talked a lot in his sleep,' she said flatly.

'What about?' asked Sloan. In his book talking while asleep was a passkey to the subconscious mind.

'It was double Dutch to me,' said the Englishwoman of the Frenchman. 'Names mostly. Hercule, Jean-Paul, François – they were always cropping up.'

'Did you never ask him who they were?'

'Once,' she said in a reserved manner.

'And?'

'He moved into the second bedroom.' She clasped her hands rigidly in her lap. 'You must remember, Inspector, that he was much older than me and I was his second wife.'

'That saying,' put in her sister truculently, 'about it being better to be an old man's darling than a young man's slave isn't true.'

Laura Vercollas flushed. 'Let us say it was a marriage of convenience.'

'*His* convenience,' added Anne Pickford tartly.

'What happened next?' asked Crosby, who was still a bachelor.

'The hotel proprietor sent for the doctor. I explained about Louis's illness and showed him all the medicines he had been having for it. He said that since we were strangers in Corbeaux he would telephone our doctor in Huisselot.'

'Then what?'

'At first everything was all right – well, straightforward anyway. I saw the undertaker and so forth and went to have a look at the cemetery – the French make rather a thing of their cemeteries.'

Sloan nodded. Even he had heard of *pompe funèbre*.

'It was outside the town and I couldn't find Louis's map

in the car, but I got there in the end.' She looked at the two policemen. 'There was no point in my taking him back to Huisselot. It hadn't been his home town or anything, and when I came to think of it I didn't even know where his parents and sister were buried. It had never cropped up, and in any case he was a very secretive man.'

'Quite so,' said Sloan.

'All I knew was their names – Henri Georges and Clothilde Marie. The sister was Clémence . . .' Her voice trailed away as if she had just remembered something.

'What is it?' asked Sloan sharply.

'Nothing.' She shook her head. 'I arranged the funeral and ordered some of those marble *éternelles* that aren't allowed in England, and then . . .'

'Then?' prompted Sloan.

'Then the doctor said that there would have to be a post-mortem after all. All of his sleeping draught had gone, you see.'

'That's when they found out about the narcotic poisoning?' said Sloan soberly.

She nodded.

'Didn't the fools think about suicide?' said Crosby, forgetting all about the professional *entente cordiale* that was supposed to exist between national police forces.

'There was no note,' said Laura Vercollas with the air of one repeating a well-rehearsed list. 'There had been no threats to end his life at any time. He wasn't in pain, and generally speaking physically ill people don't do it. To say nothing,' she added painfully, 'of its being a funny time and place to choose – the first night in a strange hotel in a strange town.'

'Looks black, doesn't it,' agreed Crosby ingenuously.

'Louis wasn't exactly poor either.' Laura Vercollas

apparently couldn't resist piling Pelion upon Ossa. 'That interested the French police a lot.'

'I'll bet,' said the Constable warmly.

'That's all very well,' said Laura Vercollas with spirit, 'but I didn't put that sleeping draught into the wine or the soup, no matter what anyone says.'

Had Crosby been French he might have said '*Bravo*' to that. Instead he looked distinctly mournful. 'They've got everything on a plate, though, haven't they?'

'A strange hotel in a strange room,' said Sloan slowly, 'and yet your husband found it easily enough.'

'He had a map.'

'No,' said Sloan quietly. 'You couldn't find the map, could you?'

She stared at him.

'And the only mistake he made in getting to the hotel was directing you up a one-way street.'

'Ye . . . es,' she said uncertainly.

'Streets that have been two-way can be made one-way.'

'What do you mean?'

'When you mentioned your husband's parents' names just now,' said Sloan swiftly, 'you were going to say something else.'

'It was nothing, Inspector. Only a coincidence.'

'Coincidence and circumstantial evidence sometimes go hand in hand,' said Sloan sternly, hoping that he might be forgiven by an unknown number of defence counsels for picking one of their best lines.

'It was when I was in the cemetery,' said Laura Vercollas. 'I wandered about a bit, as one does, and I just happened to notice a tombstone to another husband and wife called Henri Georges and Clothilde Marie, that's all. Not the same surname. It was just a coincidence.'

'And Clémence?' asked Sloan softly.

She shook her head. 'There was a Clémence but in another part of the ceme—' She stopped and stared at him.

'Madame Vercollas,' he said, 'think carefully. You arrived in Corbeaux after dark.'

'Yes.'

'You yourself went into the hotel and arranged the room. Not your husband.'

'Yes.'

'You had your meal not in the dining-room but in your bedroom.'

'Yes.'

'Who answered the door to the waiter who brought it up?'

'I did.'

'Did he see your husband?'

'No. He was in the bathroom when he came.'

'So no one in Corbeaux actually saw your husband?'

'No one.'

'Did that not strike you as very strange?'

'I hadn't thought about it.'

Sloan watched her face intently. 'Had your husband ever mentioned Corbeaux in the past?'

'He never mentioned the past at all, Inspector,' responded Laura Vercollas.

'The Occupation?'

'He wouldn't talk about the war at all except to say that he wanted to forget it.'

'So he might,' said Sloan vigorously. 'And he succeeded, didn't he? Except perhaps,' he added meaningfully, 'when he was asleep.'

'Those names, you mean?'

'Hercule, Jean-Paul, François,' said Sloan.

'And the doctor,' put in Crosby.

'Madam,' said Sloan, 'you told us the address of the hotel, didn't you?'

'Yes, I did,' she replied quickly. 'It was le Coq d'Or, Place Dr Jacques Colliard . . . Place Dr Jacques Colliard.' She stiffened. 'Inspector, there was a plaque in the square. I noticed it particularly.'

'Yes?' said Sloan into the sudden silence that had fallen in the neat sitting-room in suburban Berebury.

Madame Vercollas's voice had sunk to a whisper. 'It said, "Place Dr Jacques Colliard, Martyr de la Résistance".'

'The doctor,' said Crosby, almost under his breath.

'If what I am suggesting is so,' said Sloan carefully, 'there will be other memorials too. Such men are not forgotten in France.'

She moistened her lips. 'You mean Louis arranged to go back to Corbeaux to die? But why didn't he just . . .'

Sloan put the thought delicately: 'Perhaps he wouldn't have been welcome.'

She looked up.

'Perhaps,' he went on, 'if they had known in Corbeaux who he was they wouldn't have had him in their churchyard . . .'

'Are you saying, Inspector, he might have betrayed those men?'

'They were hard times in France,' said Sloan obliquely. 'No one knows what sort of unimaginable pressure . . .'

'The names he couldn't stop dreaming about.'

'The Gestapo,' said Sloan evenly, 'might have gone on a "shopping expedition", so to speak, that he would have found it hard to resist. Who are we to judge, madam? We are too young to know.'

'It would explain how he knew the way in the dark,' she said.

'And why he would never come to England,' said

Anne Pickford intelligently, the teapot still in her hand.

Crosby looked puzzled.

'Vercollas wouldn't have been his real name and he couldn't have got a passport,' she said.

Laura Vercollas was sitting very still. 'Inspector, if those names that Louis couldn't stop remembering in his sleep are on the Corbeaux war memorial, the French police will have to think again, won't they?'

'They will.' Sloan relaxed. 'There's something you mustn't say to them, though, madam.'

'What's that?'

'*Honi soit qui mal y pense.*'

Blue Upright

'GOOD MORNING, SIR.' The hall porter acknowledged Henry Tyler's arrival with his usual slightly inclined bow. 'Sir Coningsby asked me to say that when you came he would be in the library.'

Henry nodded, left his umbrella in the stand made from an old shell-case and went inside the building which housed the Mordaunt Club. He was appreciative, as always, of the prevailing calm there.

In spite of the political overtones of his name – his father had been a great admirer of Benjamin Disraeli – it was the fact that the Mordaunt Club was close – as Lady Bracknell might have put it – to the greater London termini that was now so helpful to Sir Coningsby Falconer. He could walk to the Mordaunt Club from the railway station and thus save himself the expense of a cab. And in these hard times, this was important.

Henry Tyler, who was his host today, went up to the library to find Sir Coningsby with whom he had been wont to have lunch on the first Tuesday in the month ever since Henry had been back at the Foreign Office in London. In happier days Sir Coningsby had been in the habit of combining their monthly meeting with visits to his wine merchant, his hatter and his bootmaker in St James's Street and his barber and cheese-merchant in Jermyn Street.

These were errands of a palmier past. The only people

whom Sir Coningsby visited in London in these sadder days were his accountants. Henry Tyler was an old enough friend to be able to enquire how things were without upsetting the luncheon atmosphere.

'Pretty bad up to Monday and a hell of a lot worse since,' said the baronet tersely.

Henry Tyler had been in the diplomatic service long enough, too, to be able to raise an enquiring eyebrow and convey sympathy at one and the same time without saying anything at all.

'Honestly, I didn't think they could possibly have got any worse, Henry, not after everything . . .'

Henry nodded sympathetically. He knew – where the casual acquaintance might not – that Sir Coningsby's troubles stemmed from an unlucky involvement in not one but two failed syndicates at Lloyd's of London. As the losses of the insurance and re-insurance syndicates had spiralled upwards, so had the fortunes of the house of Falconer of Almstone in the County of Calleshire spiralled – not to say plummeted – downwards.

'Just as I thought I was beginning to see the light at the end of the tunnel, too,' said Sir Coningsby.

'It was another train coming the other way, was it?' postulated Henry Tyler not unsympathetically.

'Caught me a real side-swipe, I can tell you,' said Sir Coningsby, mixing his metaphors with abandon. 'Oh, thank you. Yes, a decent sherry would go down very well . . .' He groaned. 'I've told 'em all at home that I've had to give up alcohol on doctor's orders . . . Dammit, Henry, there's no need to laugh like that. How would you like it if you'd had to sell your cellar?'

'I shouldn't,' said Henry unrepentantly, 'but abstinence is said to be good for the liver, you know, as well as the soul.'

'That's all very fine and large,' said Coningsby Falconer plaintively, 'though I shouldn't have minded so much if I'd been a proper rake-hell and had some fun for my money. You know, the Hell-Fire Club and all that. Losing one's inheritance on the throw of a dice or the turn of a card has – well, a certain panache about it.'

'You did have some fun,' said Henry briskly. 'And you did lose on a wager.'

Sir Coningsby wasn't listening. He was looking round at the portraits on the walls of the Mordaunt Club. 'I bet some of those fellows up there had a real run for their money. Some of 'em 've got quite a glint in their eyes.'

'Sir John Mordaunt was as hard-working a parliamentarian in his day as you could hope to find,' said Henry Tyler.

'That's all very well,' grumbled Sir Coningsby gently, 'but . . .' He was diverted by the arrival of the waiter.

'All right then,' said Henry. 'Tell me, what's gone wrong now?'

His friend took a sip of sherry. 'You know that since our troubles we've had to take in lodgers?'

'Having well-heeled visitors pay for the privilege of staying at the Lodge and fishing in one of the best chalk streams in the country,' observed Henry mildly, 'ought not in my book to be described as taking in lodgers.'

'Mother doesn't like it.'

'That may be the kernel of the matter,' agreed Henry, who had met old Lady Falconer, 'but it's not the same thing.'

'Oh, all right, then,' said Coningsby, aggrieved, 'it is fun having people one knows down for the fishing and it's no fun at all having people one doesn't know – and wouldn't want to know . . .'

Aye, thought Henry to himself, there was the rub.

'. . . swarming all over the house and staying for dinner.'

'Into the bargain,' said Henry.

'Oh, it isn't a bargain,' said Sir Coningsby a trifle naïvely. 'It costs a bomb. That's the whole idea.'

'So what went wrong, then? No fish?'

The baronet looked pained. 'Of course there were fish, Henry. You know that. The Alm's pretty well the finest trout river in the whole of the south of England, let alone Calleshire.'

'All right, then,' said Henry Tyler, who, in his time in the Foreign Office had been equally patient with rebelling tribesmen, righteous economists and petty dictators too. 'I'll buy it. The visitors didn't know how to catch trout?'

'Wrong again.' Sir Coningsby drained his schooner of sherry before he answered. 'The one that mattered knew very well how to go about fly-fishing for brown trout. He'd even brought a Blue Upright with him . . .'

Henry raked through his memory. 'A trout fly?'

'Pale peacock-quill body,' said Coningsby lugubriously, 'and a blue dun cock. The fish loved it.'

'I'm glad there was some happiness about,' said Henry.

Even mild sarcasm was wasted on Coningsby in his present frame of mind. 'Oh, the fellow could fish all right. He was the last one I'd have suspected.'

Since this said more about Coningsby Falconer than it did about the fisher, Henry once again enquired what had gone wrong.

He only got an oblique answer.

'You know my mother, don't you, old chap?'

'I do.' Henry Tyler had been taught at school that it was grammatically permissible for verbs to remain unqualified by an adverb. He thought this one of those occasions.

'Sheila had to go down to Devon to see her people this weekend so Mother stood in as hostess.'

'Surely she would have enjoyed doing that?' Presiding in one's son's house in the absence of a daughter-in-law didn't sound too arduous to Henry. A lot of dowagers he knew would have given their eye-teeth for the chance.

'Oh, yes, she enjoyed it all right,' said Sir Coningsby gloomily. 'I just had the one problem with her.'

Henry Tyler regarded his old friend with affection. Actually Coningsby had had no end of problems with his mother from childhood onwards but hadn't ever recognized them as such.

'You see, Henry, we just can't get her to see how bad things are. She thinks we should carry on as if everything's all right and it isn't.'

'No,' agreed Henry. 'It isn't.' Nevertheless he applauded the spirit that did not admit to difficulties. 'What did she do?'

'Show the flag. You know, carry on as if these people were her own guests . . .'

'That would have been what they wanted, too, wouldn't it?'

'Oh, yes, she went down a bomb with them,' he said pallidly. 'One especially. The man who fished with the Blue Upright.'

'So?'

'So she did as she always did at a big dinner party and put on her pearls.'

'I should have thought the guests would have liked that, too.'

'They did.' Sir Coningsby followed Henry out of the library and down to the Mordaunt Club dining-room. 'One in particular. Mind you, they're pretty famous ones. They're not Falconer pearls. She had 'em from her father. Perfectly graded. Took years to collect and match.'

'Even I've heard of them,' agreed Henry, to hurry the story along.

'Bit of a sore point with Sheila and me, those pearls,' said Coningsby.

'Really?'

'I don't mind telling you, Henry,' he leaned forward confidentially, 'because you don't talk.'

'Telling me what?' asked Henry, who had been paid to listen to sundry tribesmen, economists and dictators.

'About the pearls.'

'What about them, man? Is your mother going to leave them out of the family or something?'

'No, of course not, Henry.' The baronet looked quite shocked. 'What on earth could have given you that idea? Oh, the steak and kidney pudding, please . . . No, what got us is that Mother wouldn't let us raise money on them to get us out of this Lloyd's business.'

'And she could?'

'Could have,' amended Sir Coningsby. 'But wouldn't. Said her father wouldn't have liked them to be used for that. He had a good head for business, you know.'

'Yes, well . . .' Henry forbore to say anything about Sir Coningsby's business head.

'I tell you, Henry, we – Sheila and I – thought it was the same as being in one of those prisons built like the inside of the top of a wine bottle upside-down . . .' He waved his fork in a graphic gesture. 'You know . . . where they had a stream dripping within earshot but out of reach until the prisoner died of thirst.'

'An *oubliette*,' supplied Henry.

'That's it.' He laid the fork back on the table. 'Those pearls could have saved us like the water could have saved the prisoner . . .'

'If he could have got his hands on it,' pointed out Henry unkindly.

'Not that that matters now . . .'

'Why not?' In Henry's not inconsiderable experience, troubles did not roll away as simply as that.

'Didn't I tell you? One of the people staying for the fishing stole them.'

'Your mother's pearls?'

'Gone.' Sir Coningsby looked even more lugubrious. 'Oh, the police are pretty sure who had them but they can't prove anything.'

'He with the Blue Upright?'

'Him. We all had to be fingerprinted after the ebony case with the pearls in disappeared. Mother didn't like that.'

Henry hadn't imagined that she would.

'Blue Upright turned out to be one of a pair of international jewel thieves.'

'What did the other one fish with? A February Red?'

'I didn't ask,' said Sir Coningsby with dignity. 'I never saw him. He stayed at the Dog and Duck down in the village. They found his fingerprints in his room there. That was after the police worked out how the pair of 'em got away with the pearls.'

'Tell me,' invited Henry.

'Blue Upright takes them from Ma's room while she's asleep, puts them in his tackle bag and goes down to the river first thing . . .'

'Before she knows they've gone? Oh, by the way, what'll you have to drink?'

'I thought you'd never ask,' said his friend, taking the wine list. 'Yes. Said he wanted the early light.'

'Since they're still missing I take it the river bank has been searched?'

'Ratty and Mole couldn't have done a better job,' said Coningsby, who had had a proper grounding in English literature. 'That's when they went looking for the other fellow. Downstream, of course.'

'As I remember, the river picks up steam below you, doesn't it?'

'Goes straight down from my beat into the old mill pool opposite the Dog and Duck,' said Coningsby. He tapped the wine list. 'The Gamay would go well, I think, if it's all right with you, old chap . . .'

'Meantime Blue Upright comes back indoors asking what the fuss is all about?'

'He even had the nerve to come back with a couple of quite decent brown trout,' growled Coningsby, 'while his pal further downstream . . .'

'Whom I shall call "February Red",' murmured Henry.

'. . . was picking up the ebony box from the mill pool with his net.'

'The Dog and Duck is reckoned to be a fishing inn, isn't it?' observed Henry.

Coningsby Falconer scowled. 'The police think he – Blue Upright – chucked the box in the Alm from the little bridge and just let it float downriver to his accomplice.'

'He whom we are referring to as February Red,' put in Henry helpfully.

'Actually, Henry, I tried it myself later with some bits of wood and it worked. Like Pooh-sticks, though I don't think the police chappie knew what I was talking about . . .'

'No,' agreed Henry thoughtfully. 'Tell me about this ebony box.'

'It was something the mater had picked up in Ceylon on her honeymoon. Quite small but beautifully carved and all that.' He roused himself to recollect yet another grievance. 'She was very fond of that box – sentimental associations and so forth.' He plunged his face into the glass of Gamay and said: 'If you ask me she minds as much about the box as she does about the pearls she won't let us raise the ante on.'

'Funny things, women . . .'

'Sheila's all right,' said Sheila's husband stoutly. 'She's been an absolute brick all through our troubles. Oh, thank you, waiter. Yes, I'll have all the vegetables please . . .'

'Oh, no, you won't,' said Henry suddenly. 'At least, not just yet. Waiter, take Sir Coningsby's steak and kidney pudding back to the kitchen and keep it hot. He's got an urgent phone call to make . . .'

'I have?' said the bewildered baronet, watching his luncheon disappear with an expression of schoolboy regret on his face.

'You will ring the Calleshire police at once,' instructed Henry Tyler, sometime Foreign Office official in Mauritius, 'and ask them to institute an immediate search of the river bed below the bridge . . .'

'The bridge . . .'

'Where I am pretty sure they will find a small ebony box containing your mother's pearls, Pooh-sticks notwithstanding. No, on second thoughts leave that last bit out . . .'

'But . . .' spluttered Coningsby, who was taking the precaution of finishing his wine before that, too, was put on 'hold'.

'Tell them instead that ebony wood doesn't float.'

'It doesn't?'

'It's too heavy. It sinks.'

'So those blighters waited in the wrong place, did they?' Coningsby's face cleared. 'Just goes to show we can all make mistakes, doesn't it?'

Devilled Dip

'YOU,' announced his wife portentously, 'are going to be the life and soul of today's events.'

The man, who was known as Ant, nodded, unmoved. 'Oh, yes?'

'That's what it says here,' she said, looking a little doubtful herself.

'Me?'

'You.' She rustled the paper. 'Honest.' Indeed, on the surface the idea that her husband should be the life and soul of any events did seem an unlikely thing to be going to happen. Especially as it would have been quite difficult to imagine Madge's husband, Anthony, being the life and soul of any gathering. His calculated unobtrusiveness was actually part and parcel of his working stock-in-trade and a more insignificant-looking man would have been hard to find.

'Arcturus is the favourite for the two thirty,' he murmured, almost to himself. 'Going firm to hard.'

Where his wife favoured horoscopes, he studied the turf.

'Something, Ant,' insisted his wife, still reading aloud, 'connected with you is going to happen today that will change someone's life.'

He nodded at that, too, similarly unsurprised. What he did frequently changed someone's life. At the very least, it made them more careful afterwards. For ever afterwards.

He went back to the racing page. Time was when he and his wife had tried to combine their separate interests but horosocopes had proved an even more uncertain way to racing success than the study of form and now by tacit consent they each pursued their own separate avocations.

'Aquarius,' she said, running her fat finger further down the page. 'It says here that today'll be a day to remember.'

'Arcturus nearly won the Almstone Cup last week at Calleford,' he said, shoving the tub of margarine off the sports pages and on to the newspaper's gossip column. He reached for the marmalade jar. Madge would continue, he knew, without any encouragement from him until she had taken in every aspect of the day's horoscope.

'You'll have to be ever so careful,' she said, 'until midnight.'

'I'm always careful, aren't I?' He piled the marmalade on to the bread with the absent-minded amplitude of a thin man. 'Harry's Dive is the favourite, though.'

'Funny name for a horse,' said Madge who took Sagittarius and Capricorn in her stride every morning.

'Out of Cellar by Night Life.' If he, Ant, were ever to own a race-horse he would call it Wallet out of Back Pocket by Sleight of Hand. A real traditionalist, Ant deeply regretted the new fashion of visitors to this country wearing a purse strung round their waists like a kangaroo-pouch. He was, he felt, a little too set in his ways to learn new methods of being what Chaucer would have called a 'cut-purse'.

'What do you think she means?' she pondered.

'Who?'

She tapped the newspaper. 'This woman here. Madame Whatyoucallit.'

'Dunno.'

'She's very clever.' For years Madge had followed the daily horoscope of a man whose improbably good-looking features, including a neatly trimmed beard, had adorned the top of his newspaper piece. Of late though she – or, rather, the newspaper proprietor – had switched her allegiance to the astrological prognostications of a woman whose gypsy-like appearance was underlined by a head-scarf and dangling ear-rings.

Ant suspected the column was still being written by the same hand. Madge, however, had a touching faith in the predictions of the unknown writer and no faith at all in anything or anyone else – but especially not in her husband, Anthony.

'Someone, Ant,' she quoted, 'will this day owe you an immense debt of gratitude.'

He grunted at the sheer unlikeliness of that. Most of the people from whom he made his living had good cause to regret their brief encounter with him rather than the other way round. And the briefer the encounter, the better, from Ant's point of view. The length of their exchange wasn't so important to his victims since he was not a violent man and never had been. And he certainly wasn't in the habit of getting caught.

This last may have had something to do with the fact that he wasn't greedy. He never did more than one job a day – after which he would make straight for the betting shop. Most of the evidence disappeared over the counter there long before the police became involved. He himself attributed his relative freedom from prosecution to luck – and to his practice of always addressing such policemen as came his way as 'Mister'. In spite of this act of *pietas* he had been arraigned from time to time and therefore took as keen an interest in the workings of the law as the Lord Chancellor himself.

He tucked into more bread and margarine now since he wasn't a drinking man either and wouldn't be having his lunch in a pub even though his working day would be spent in the city. This abstinence was not a matter of choice but the result of an innate weakness in his constitution. He couldn't take drink without his digestion being thoroughly upset.

In fact, Ant figured altogether rather low down life's totem pole. Even the name of Anthony assigned to him by a rather deaf clergyman had been a mistake. His mother – the daughter of a pig-man and brought up on a farm deep in rural Calleshire – had actually wanted him called Tantony. This had been in much the same spirit as other people called their son Benjamin in the pious hope that he would be the last of the tribe: a tantony being the last or runt of the sow's litter.

Runt really described Ant rather well. Where he was thin and had a look of permanent undernourishment about him, his wife was the reverse. She had Queen Anne legs – it would have been a kindness to call them cabriolet – but there was no understating her size. And the larger she grew, the smaller her husband seemed.

'I've got to be careful today,' she said, 'because of Uranus and Neptune.'

'Credenza's running in the three o'clock,' he countered, keeping his own end up. 'Odds on.'

'And the Sun is challenged by Mars,' she read on. 'That sounds dangerous.'

'You watch those kitchen steps . . .' he said. 'They're definitely dangerous.'

'And you watch your step, Ant . . . one day a cony'll get you instead of you getting him.'

'Never worry,' he said, draining his tea-cup. He put it down on the table without consulting the leaves. Once upon a time, when they had first married, Madge had been quite keen on reading the tea-leaves but he hadn't liked it and had said so. He wasn't a sensitive man but even so, it didn't seem quite nice: not when everyone knew that the cockney rhyming slang for 'thief' was 'tea-leaf'.

He left Madge sitting at the kitchen table still pondering on what it was that was going to happen today to make him, Ant, important in the scheme of things. 'Back teatime,' he said over his shoulder by way of farewell.

As usual, he took himself into the city centre by bus. Bus passengers were incurious fellow travellers at the best of times and Ant's total unmemorability made it even less likely that anyone would remember having seen him that or any other morning.

He slipped away from the bus stop – he was not a man who ever strode anywhere anyway – with his customary inconspicuousness and made his way to the concourse in front of the cathedral where the fountain played. This spot invariably attracted the tourists on whom Ant preyed.

Those who congregated there usually spent their time throwing coins into the fountain's basin – an action which Ant thought was definitely wasteful and probably pagan in origin but for which he was grateful as it showed him just where his victims kept their small change if not their big money.

He watched the little crowd while he selected his victim. His first choice was a man hung about with expensive cameras and he was just trying to identify which of the bulges in his pocket was wallet and which new film when a woman waved at the man and he moved away. Ant could have followed for the kill but he didn't. Like a tiger he preferred his prey to be solitary – and with no likelihood of having anyone keeping a weather eye on him or her.

His next choice was a younger man but more obviously from overseas. That was a plus point in Ant's book. Those unfamiliar with the British scene were less likely to lead a hue and cry or to know their way about the complex pattern of medieval streets round the old cathedral.

This fellow was trying to photograph the famous view of the cathedral's ancient west front edged by the curve of the fountain and he was making a thorough job of it. Twice he adjusted his stance just as Ant was equally carefully judging his own distance from the chap's back pocket.

Ant waited until a little gaggle of other tourists turned in his own direction and then walked towards them. As they drew level with the photographer Ant stepped behind him, as if to let the others proceed and with consummate skill – just as they had passed him but were still sheltering him from the view of anyone on their side – he lifted the man's wallet from his pocket.

It was very skilfully done indeed and he doubted whether the man had felt a thing. Ant did not move away in undue haste – that would have lacked artistry. Instead, he carried on past his victim, in the direction it would have seemed he had always been planning to proceed. He crossed the cathedral concourse, palming his prize into one of his own especially capacious 'poacher's' pockets, and to all intents and purposes making for the old coaching inn at the corner.

He did indeed enter the bar there but left immediately by another door. Within a minute he was back in the street – a much busier one than before – and heading straight for his favourite betting establishment.

While it would have been true to say that his ear was cocked for any sound of a chase, it was equally fair to record that he was not worried about it – and that he had, too, completely forgotten the gypsy's warning so carefully spelled out for him by Madge that morning.

Whether it would have made any difference if he had been more careful at that point or whether predestination really did have a part to play in the eternal scheme of things Ant never did know.

All he knew was that the shout of warning from the pavement came too late to save him from being in the direct path of the lorry which came hurtling down the road, careering all over the carriageway, its driver slumped down unconscious over the wheel.

The House Surgeon at the hospital was young and still idealistic. Confronted by one dead man and one dying one, he promptly instituted a search for organ donor cards. The lorry driver hadn't been carrying one but inside the wallet in Ant's pocket there was a signed card giving very clear permission for any tissue to be removed after death. That the name was not Ant's name but that of another – a visitor from a younger country – was not apparent to the hands at the hospital which dispatched the battered form – already beyond aid, as the House Physician duly recorded – to what is euphemistically known as the non-recovery theatre.

Tissue typing was set in motion even as someone sought the Coroner's permission to do so. Attempts were made, too, to get in touch with a remote homestead on the edge of the Nullarbor Plain.

No one, however, made any effort to take the sad news to Ant's wife, Madge, nowhere near as far away and still sitting over Ant's horoscope trying to figure out exactly how her husband – nondescript to a fault – could ever be the life and soul of the day's events.

Or for it to be a day to remember.

The Misjudgement of Paris

HENRY MOLLAND gave his wife the news during dinner. He chose the moment with his customary care, since he did not want her mind deflected in any way from her cooking. Waiting until they'd finished their first course of steak with a perfectly judged *béarnaise* sauce and after Mary had placed some home-made apple pie before him, he told her that the final interviews for the post of the firm's general manager, UK, were to be held this week in Paris.

'Paris!' she exclaimed, adding urgently, 'When?'

'Thursday.'

'Thursday? That means ...' Mary began to look extremely thoughtful. 'Do you know, Henry, I think if I really concentrate, I could finish Lucy's birthday present for you to take over with you.'

Henry nodded. 'I thought that was what you would say.'

Mary Molland was an expert at the almost lost craft of smocking and had been working on the most beautiful of nightdresses for weeks. 'Lucy'll just have to put the hem up herself, that's all.'

Since Lucy's doting father considered Lucy capable of absolutely everything, he did not feel this to be a worry.

'Why Paris?' asked Mary presently. 'Do you mind just clearing the table, dear. I think I'll do a little more stitching before the light goes ...'

'Well, we are an international firm after all, and the Board are meeting in Paris anyway. There's a big trade exhibition on this week.'

'M'm . . .'

'And anyway I think they want to see how the candidates get on without support staff – secretaries and so forth . . .'

'Wives, you mean.'

'Them too.' Henry stacked the dishes from their meal methodically on to a tray, challenging himself to take them to the kitchen in one journey.

'And who else is being interviewed?' enquired Mary, adding loyally: 'Not that they'll stand a chance against you.'

Henry laughed. 'Don't you believe it. There's Smeaton and Carmichael and Bullock. Mustn't underestimate Bullock, he's a clever lad even though he's still a bit wet behind the ears.'

'And who will get the job, then, dear?' She added hastily, 'If you don't, I mean.'

'One of the young Turks, I expect. Not me, anyway. Much too long in the tooth.'

'You've been with the company longest.'

'That's the trouble, old age.'

'Well,' said Mary briskly, ignoring this last like the good wife she was, 'at least Lucy'll get her birthday present in good time. You never know with these foreign posts, do you? Give her my love.'

In the event, the actual delivery of his daughter's birthday present turned out to be a little more problematical than Henry had expected. It transpired that Lucy, while working in Paris during the day, had her evenings bespoken by a young man called Jules.

'You'll love him, Daddy, when you meet him.'

'Good,' said Lucy's father, who had met a great many of Lucy's admirers in his time. It emerged, though, that

155

his meeting with Jules was not to be quite yet.

'Your birthday present . . .' said Henry firmly, 'on which your mother has been labouring for weeks, is here at my hotel and I am going home on Thursday evening.'

'Daddy, what about my coming to your hotel for breakfast? I'm not busy at breakfast time.'

Henry said sternly that he was glad to hear it and would expect her at seven o'clock the next morning and not a moment later because he had a busy day ahead of him.

'*Alors, demain, à sept heures, Papa,*' said Lucy sweetly, and went to get ready for Jules.

Henry on his part also had the next day to prepare for. He and Smeaton, Carmichael and Bullock foregathered briefly in the hotel bar after getting their marching orders for the next day.

Bullock, anxious to maintain his standing as the youngest – and therefore the most vigorous – of the candidates and to demonstrate the qualities of leadership said to be sought by all appointments boards proposed they all had a night on the tiles together.

'No use wasting a stag night in Paris, now is there?'

Smeaton, whose academic qualifications were impeccable and in his own view quite unassailable too, agreed to join him. 'What about you two others?'

It was well known to them all that Henry Molland had started with the company as a grease monkey and thus had only ever had 'hands on' experience – moreover, he had no 'alphabet soup' after his name either. He was therefore no challenge to a high-flyer like Smeaton who could afford to be magnanimous.

'You'd better count me out anyway,' murmured Carmichael. 'I thought I'd just run over a few figures for tomorrow over dinner in my room.'

Carmichael was the workaholic of the quartet and in any

case thought zeal ought to be a prerequirement of the promotion fast lane.

'What about you then, Molland?' challenged Bullock. 'Or do you want a quiet evening with a good balance sheet, too?'

'A quiet evening with a good menu will suit me very well,' returned Henry equably. He certainly wasn't going to waste it working, belonging as he did to the school of thought that held that Rudyard Kipling's poem 'If' had a lot to answer for and Dr Samuel Smiles' books on 'Self-Help' even more.

Besides, the hotel had a stately dining-room that was a cross between the Palace of Versailles and the old Euston station, which he had every intention of exploring.

'It's no good your thinking the Board will be eating there, too, Molland,' said Bullock maliciously. 'They've all been invited to a reception at the British Embassy to do with this Trade Fair.'

'I know that,' said Henry. 'I shouldn't be dining here otherwise.'

He was glad, though, that he was. As well as being built on classical lines the hotel dining-room had a memorable *carte* to match it. He telephoned Mary, assured her of the safe arrival of himself and Lucy's new nightdress, and then settled down to a good meal and an early night.

Seven o'clock the next morning found him rested, bathed, shaved and dressed – and waiting in the foyer of the hotel.

'Daddy, darling . . .'

Suddenly he was being kissed by a very elegant young lady indeed. He squared his shoulders and led the way into the dining-room. They were, in fact, the first arrivals and were led to a window table.

'I've got lots to tell you . . .' began Lucy. And so she

had although Henry noticed that nearly all of it seemed to include a mention of Jules' name. Lovesick, though, Henry was happy to observe, Lucy wasn't. Croissants were waved away in favour of a proper English breakfast.

'The French don't understand morning food,' she declared, agreeing to the waiter's offer of more toast. There was never any shortage of waiters when Lucy ate.

The dining-room filled up as they talked and talked. Out of the corner of his eye Henry saw the members of the selection board trickle in and then Carmichael – looking drawn. A long while after that Bullock came in – looking like a man who has had a night on the tiles – and addressed himself to a pot of coffee. He waved away a basket of croissants in quite a different manner from Lucy.

Of Smeaton there was no sign.

'Darling, that was lovely but I must go or I'll be late . . .' Lucy started to push back her chair. At least three waiters decided she needed help with this operation and rushed forward. She thanked them with great charm and Henry got up to go with her to the door.

'Your mother will never forgive either of us if we forget this,' said Henry, handing over a parcel wrapped in tissue paper.

'Oh, my goodness, no.' Lucy stood still in the middle of the dining-room while she unwrapped it. As the tissue paper fell away the most exquisite of hand-smocked night-dresses was revealed to the entire dining-room. His daughter reached up and kissed Henry on the cheek and then swept out, nightdress and all.

The young Turks never stood a chance.

Her Indoors

'I'M AFRAID that all we've got to go on in the way of clues is in here, Sloan.' Superintendent Leeyes picked up the neatly parcelled book on his desk and handed it across to Detective Inspector Sloan. 'And that's not much.'

'Yes, sir,' said Sloan, taking the book from his superior officer with some reluctance.

'I read it all through myself yesterday,' said Leeyes loftily. 'Very well written, I thought, if that's any help.'

The book felt well bound anyway, by the feel of it, and was rather heavy. Sloan said, 'Thank you, sir,' aloud – and rather more under his breath.

'The Assistant Chief Constable says that nevertheless everything you'll need is there and he should know.'

'Yes, sir.'

'Educated chap, the ACC,' sniffed the Superintendent, who disapproved of the man himself and of his classical education in equal parts. 'All the background you'll ever possibly need is there, too.'

'I'm sure,' echoed Sloan dutifully. He was really too busy to enter into even the spirit of this sort of assignment let alone the reality. 'You say, sir, that we don't even know the lady's name?'

'Not her Christian name. That's why – strictly for the purposes of this inquiry alone – we're calling her Mrs P. We only know her husband's and her son's names for certain – and her daughter's, of course, though the daughter's name doesn't get mentioned any more after what happened . . . and I for one am not surprised about that.'

'Portrait turned to the wall?' suggested Sloan delicately.

'You could say that, Sloan. In a manner of speaking, anyway. Not that that helps us with the mother's name.'

'Mrs P's age, sir? Is that known?'

'I reckon we could have what you might call an educated guess at that, Sloan.'

Detective Inspector Sloan got out his notebook. A guess was better than nothing.

'Mr P,' pronounced the Superintendent weightily, 'was a doddering old fool and tedious with it.'

'So she killed him?' asked Sloan, anxious to get on with another case.

'Certainly not, Sloan. He was killed by their daughter's boyfriend.'

'Mrs P might have been younger than her husband, then?' suggested Sloan, his train of thought going off at a tangent to another scenario that included toy-boys and gigolos.

'Well, she might,' conceded Leeyes, 'but remember she did have a grown-up son.' He grunted. 'Actually now I come to think about it, the son seemed to me to have been about the only one in the whole set-up who behaved like a grown-up.'

Sloan sighed. 'That'll be a great help, that will, sir.' Juvenile behaviour in those old enough to know better was a perennial cross that all policemen had to learn to bear with what grace they could.

'Even though he was nearly as free with his advice as his father, and that's saying something.'

Detective Inspector Sloan was beginning to feel quite some sympathy towards the unidentified Mrs P.

160

'Even,' rumbled on Leeyes, 'his sister thought he was getting like a preacher.'

'Pointing morals?'

'Saying one thing and doing another,' said Leeyes tartly.

'Ah.'

'Mind you, Mrs P can't have been all that young, Sloan, because the son must have been – well, say early twenties like his sister's boyfriend.'

'The boyfriend who murdered Mr P?' Sloan tried to get at least one thing clear in his mind.

The Superintendent raised an admonitory hand. 'I don't think we can use the word murder in connection with that particular death, Sloan. It wouldn't be wise. Not just yet.'

'No? But, sir, I thought the old man was stabbed or something?'

'So he was, Sloan, but the killer just lunged at the curtain. We don't know for certain – that is, a clever lawyer would be able to cast plenty of doubt around – that the killer knew Mr P would be standing there on the other side of it at the exact time that the curtain was stabbed. There's no real evidence, you see.'

'So the friend just went around stabbing at curtains, then, did he?'

'Well, he was a bit of a funny lad,' admitted Leeyes enigmatically. 'There's a family history there that people have gone into a lot . . .'

'The Crown Prosecution Service wouldn't have liked that.' Daniel M'Naghten may have been long dead and gone but he and his Rules on criminal insanity still cast their shadow over the successful prosecution of the mentally unbalanced who came to judgement.

'The Crown Prosecution didn't like any of it,' said Superintendent Leeyes, adding vigorously: 'and as far as I'm concerned, Sloan, you can drop the word "service" in connection with anything to do with them. They may be a lot of odd things but service they most definitely aren't.'

'Yes, sir.' Detective Inspector Sloan kept his peace and let this particular bee circle round in the Superintendent's bonnet without comment.

'Not that the son's friend is our concern anyway.' Superintendent Leeyes straightened his shoulders.

'No?'

'No. He was in enough trouble on his own account and he's already had more written about him than practically any other man alive.' The Superintendent waved his finger. 'Just you remember that it's the character of Mrs P that the Assistant Chief Constable wanted my – wants your – opinion on – your opinion as a working detective, that is.'

'I see, sir.' Detective Inspector Sloan was only too happy to try to get back to the point even if this was the oddest job that had come his way in many a long year in the Calleshire Police Force. 'So,' he said patiently, 'we do know that she was the wife of an old man and the mother of a young one and therefore roughly middle-aged?'

'Yes,' admitted Leeyes grudgingly. 'I don't think that that can be other than right.' The Superintendent would, they both knew, have faulted Sloan's reasoning if he possibly could have done from sheer force of habit.

'But I take it, sir, that we do know quite a lot about her husband before he was murd— killed?'

'Not really. Except that he was keen on amateur dramatics – bit of an actor himself in his youth and something of a critic, otherwise . . .'

Sloan waited.

'Otherwise, we only really know him by how he behaved and by what he said,' amplified Superintendent Leeyes carefully.

'When you come to think of it, sir, I dare say that's the

only way anyone ever knows anyone else anyway.'

'Very possibly, Sloan.' The Superintendent ignored this tempting philosophical by-way and said: 'It's all down in that book though.'

Sloan stared at the fat tome. He'd never have time to wade through all that. Hoping that there were no feminists within earshot he asked: 'What was Mr P's occupation?' The feminists, he knew, would argue that Mrs P shouldn't be assessed on the nature of her husband's way of earning his livelihood but he would have to make a start somewhere or he'd be here all night . . .

'That,' harrumphed Leeyes, 'seems to have been disputed. Civil servant probably but the daughter's boyfriend insisted he was only a fishmonger.'

'Going to marry above her station, sir, was she?' divined Sloan without difficulty. Presumably Mrs P would have been pleased about that.

'Not if Mr P could help it,' said Leeyes firmly. 'You just read the case up in that book, Sloan, and see for yourself how shockingly Mr P mucked up his daughter's love life, poor girl.'

'Yes, sir.'

'Mind you, I'd have had doubts myself about her boyfriend as a future son-in-law so I dare say Mr P had, too. A right mixed-up kiddo if you ask me . . .'

'You don't think, sir, do you, that someone at the station here with family therapy experience would do better than me at this assignment? Or,' he added, since the Superintendent was more than something of a misogynist, 'even a woman? Woman Police Sergeant Perkins is very good at domestics.'

Superintendent Leeyes' response was unusually oblique. 'Now, Sloan, don't be put off by the size of that book. I tell you it's mostly background, and you won't have to read it all. Just the relevant bits. After all, the kid's only fourteen.'

'What kid?'

'Never you mind,' said Leeyes severely. 'Just you concentrate on finding out all you can about Mrs P like the Assistant Chief wants.'

'Via her husband and son?'

'There isn't anyone else – that we know about, that is.'

Detective Inspector Sloan toyed with the delicious temptation of saying to the Superintendent that if the Assistant Chief Constable wanted a miracle then he, Sloan, would have to go back home for his wand; but he thought better of it. There was, after all, not only his pension to think of but his hard-won reputation as a working detective to consider.

'I think, sir,' he reasoned carefully, 'that Mrs P was probably outwardly compliant but inwardly seething when her husband pontificated on family matters. Otherwise she'd have left him long ago.'

'Sanctimonious wasn't in it,' agreed Leeyes, 'when Mr P got going. I can tell you that. You name it and he'd give you advice on it.'

'Trying,' agreed Sloan, who knew from hard experience how irksome a ready word in a difficult police investigation could be. 'Very trying. So,' he added briskly, 'I suggest we can assume she developed coping techniques in that direction. Switched off mentally whenever he opened his mouth, I expect, or she'd have gone under.'

'There's another thing,' said Leeyes, who didn't seem to have been listening, 'as you'll see when you read what he said.' Superintendent Leeyes pointed to the book in Sloan's hand. 'Mr P wasn't the sort of man to let Mrs P pop out and borrow a cup of sugar from the people next door or ask for the loan of a screw of tea, come to that. According to him they had to be self-sufficient no matter what.'

'So,' concluded Sloan ineluctably, 'she was a good manager then, too.'

'Must have been. Her husband was very hot on good husbandry.'

'Hard done by with the housekeeping, was she, then, too, sir?'

'Shouldn't be surprised,' Leeyes said. 'But not in every way.'

'Oh?'

'Mr P was the living proof of that bit of Shakespeare's about wearing what you could afford.'

A good dress allowance, thought Sloan to himself, could have been little comfort in Mrs P's exiguous circumstances. If it was a good allowance, that is. He indicated the book. 'Do any of the family ever quote her?'

Leeyes shook his head. 'Not once that I heard about.'

That, thought the Detective Inspector to himself, could be good or bad. Mrs P might have been one of those strong silent women who said nothing memorable from choice: or, equally, was too tentative to commit herself.

'Her son did once describe her brows as chaste and unsmirched,' volunteered Leeyes unexpectedly, 'but the Assistant Chief Constable wouldn't accept that as real evidence . . .'

'Coming from the son?'

'Didn't think it was reliable enough for his son to use.'

'Hearsay from an interested party?' suggested Sloan, by now more than a trifle confused himself in the matter of sons. 'You'd have thought, sir, wouldn't you,' he added, 'that Mr P would have said something to his son like "Your mother says to wear your thick coat when it's cold".'

It was the sort of embarrassing remark that his own father had made to him when he was no longer a boy.

'More likely to have been a warning about the French,' muttered Leeyes, 'since he was so busy arranging for a friend to spy on the lad when he was in Paris.' He grimaced. 'And much good that did him.'

Sloan made one last bid for Mr P as common-or-garden *pater familias* by appealing to the Superintendent's legendary xenophobia. 'You know what Frenchmen are . . .'

'These weren't,' said Leeyes briefly.

Sloan shook his head. 'I'm afraid that she – Mrs P, that is – is proving a bit – well, difficult to catch hold of, sir, isn't she?'

'Just what the Assistant Chief Constable said himself,' said Leeyes triumphantly. 'Quite put out about it, he was when he went into it. Nebulous was the word he used.'

It wasn't the one Sloan was looking for. He thought that Mrs P must have been definite enough.

Cowed? He wasn't sure.

Talked to death by her husband and son?

Very probably.

'I reckon she was better off as widow than as wife, anyway, sir, no matter what,' he said aloud.

'That's a good point,' said Leeyes grandly.

'A bit of peace and quiet can't have come amiss, sir.' Sloan thought that Mrs P had probably dealt very early on in her marriage with what the hymn-writer had called 'the murmurings of self-will'.

'I'll tell the Assistant Chief Constable you said so,' promised Leeyes.

'I think,' said Sloan even more categorically, 'she would really have had to have been a woman who bit down hard before speaking . . .'

'That figures,' said Leeyes.

'. . . who obeyed her husband without challenging him. At least, from what you've said, sir, Mr P doesn't seem to have behaved like a man challenged on the domestic front.'

'True,' said Leeyes.

Sloan waxed a little more expansive still. 'Of course, sir, Mr P just might have been the reverse of the usual man – a saint at home and a devil abroad . . .'

'Hrrmmmph,' said Leeyes, who was inclined to take everything personally.

'But,' hurried on Sloan, 'somehow I don't think so. He sounded to have been an interfering old buzzard to me.'

The Superintendent nodded sagely. 'As character assassinations go, Sloan, that's not too bad.'

'Mrs P must have had a hard time,' said Sloan, 'all the same.'

Hard times bred a certain cast of mind in a woman; he knew that. That was more grist to the Assistant Chief Constable's mill and he said so to the Superintendent.

'He said the boy would be grateful for anything, Sloan.'

'What boy?'

'His son,' Leeyes said, adding sedulously, 'Didn't I say?'

'No, sir. You didn't.'

'It's his son who's been landed with the job, you see – his father just wanted to know if we could help and seeing as his father is the Assistant Chief Constable . . .'

'I see all right, sir, thank you,' responded Sloan stiffly. 'It's quite clear to me now.'

'You must know what it's like, Sloan,' said the Superintendent, 'when a kid can't do his homework and asks his father for help . . .'

'And his father can't do it either . . .'

'But I thought we could,' said Leeyes, who was inclined to use the Royal 'we' when it suited him.

'This Mrs P, sir,' said Sloan, weighing the heavy book in his hand consideringly. 'Do we happen to know – I mean, is it known – where she lived?'

'Oh, didn't I say that either?' murmured the Superintendent shamelessly.

'No.'

'She lived in Denmark.'

'Elsinore?' said Sloan.

'That's right. You see, it was his English homework that the ACC's son couldn't get anywhere with this week.'

'I see, sir,' said Sloan tonelessly.

'. . . and the homework was an essay on Shakespeare's *Hamlet*: "Describe Mrs Polonius given Polonius and Laertes". Quite amazing what these schoolmasters dream up, isn't it?'